CHRISTMAS
IN MY HEART

10

FOCUS ON THE FAMILY®

CHRISTMAS IN MY HEART

A TREASURY OF TIMELESS CHRISTMAS STORIES

10

compiled and edited by

JOE L. WHEELER

TYNDALE HOUSE PUBLISHERS, INC., WHEATON, ILLINOIS

Visit Tyndale's exciting Web site at www.tyndale.com

Author photo by Joel Springer © 2000. All rights reserved.

Woodcut illustrations are from the library of Joe L. Wheeler.

Designed by Jenny Swanson.

Published in association with the literary agency of Alive Communications, Inc., 7680 Goddard St., Suite 200, Colorado Springs, Colorado 80920.

Library of Congress Cataloging-in-Publication Data

Christmas in my heart/ [compiled by] Joe L. Wheeler.
  p. cm.
  ISBN 0-8423-5380-1 (10)
  1. Christmas stories, American. I. Wheeler, Joe L., date

PS648.C45C447   1992

813'.010833—dc20

Printed in the United States of America

09 08 07 06 05 04 03 02 01
10   9   8   7   6   5   4   3   2   1

DEDICATION

Very early along the way, he came into our lives.
Without his continued encouragement, without his wise
counsel, without his serving as both a buffer and a
conduit between us and publishers and editors, this great
ministry of Judeo-Christian stories just would not have
happened; he is our co-partner.

But more than all that, he is a brother—
of both spirit and soul—who loves the Lord
with every atom of his being.

As this tenth anniversary edition of Christmas in My
Heart is prepared for press, it gives me great joy to
dedicate it to the one who has done the most to help
make it all possible, our beloved agent:

GREG JOHNSON
of
Alive Communications, Inc.

CONTENTS

ACKNOWLEDGMENTS

"Anniversary," by Joseph Leininger Wheeler. Copyright © 2001. Printed by permission of the author.

"The Sheaf of Grain," by Bernadine Beatie. Published in December 1966 *Friend* magazine. Text reprinted by permission of Church of Jesus Christ of Latter Day Saints, Salt Lake City, Utah. Also published in December 17, 1970 *Primary Treasure*. Text reprinted by permission of Pacific Press Publishing Association, Nampa, Idaho. If anyone can provide knowledge of earliest publication date and publisher, as well as location of author or descendants, please send this information to Joe Wheeler (P.O. Box 1246, Conifer, CO 80433).

"A Precious Memory," by D. T. Doig. Published in December 1986 *Good Housekeeping*. Reprinted by permission of Rosalind Doig (daughter of the author).

"Lights of the Season," by P. J. Platz. Reprinted by permission of P. J. Platz (Patricia and Traci Lambrecht).

"Good Will Toward Men," by Harry Harrison Kroll. Published in December 23, 1933 *Young People's Weekly*. Text reprinted by permission of Joe Wheeler (P.O. Box 1246, Conifer, CO 80433) and David C. Cook Ministries, Colorado Springs, Colorado.

"No Man Need Walk Alone," by Seth Parker. Published in *Quiet Hour Echoes*, December 1967. If anyone can provide knowledge of the first publication source of this old story, please send this information to Joe Wheeler (P.O. Box 1246, Conifer, CO 80433).

"Terry," by Frank V. McMillan. Published in December 20, 1986 *Guide*. Reprinted by permission of Review and Herald Publishing Association and Michael McMillan (son of the author).

"Secrets of the Heart," by Pearl S. Buck. Reprinted by permission of Harold Ober Associates.

"While Shepherds Watched," by Adeline Sergeant. Published in December 1898 *Nor-West Farmer*, Winnipeg, Canada.

"Johnny Christmas," author unknown. If anyone can provide

knowledge of authorship, first publication source, and current ownership of the rights to this story, please send this information to Joe Wheeler (P.O. Box 1246, Conifer, CO 80433).

"No Room at the Inn," by Harriet Lummis Smith. Published in December 24, 1932 *Young People's Weekly*. Text reprinted by permission of Joe Wheeler (P.O. Box 1246, Conifer, CO 80433) and David C. Cook Ministries, Colorado Springs, Colorado.

"Star of Wonder," by Grace Livingston Hill. Included in *Miss Lavinia's Call and Other Stories* (Philadelphia and New York: J. B. Lippincott Company 1949). Reprinted by R. L. Munce Publishing, Inc.

"Good Old Christmas Preferred," by Anna Brownell Dunaway. Published in December 23, 1934 *Young People's Weekly*. Text reprinted by permission of Joe Wheeler (P.O. Box 1246, Conifer, CO 80433) and David C. Cook Ministries, Colorado Springs, Colorado.

"The Second Greatest Christmas Story Ever Told," by Thomas J. Burns. Reprinted with permission from the December 1989 *Reader's Digest* and the author.

"The Tree in the Window," by Margaret E. Sangster, Jr. Published in December 16, 1933 *Young People's Weekly*. Text reprinted by permission of Joe Wheeler (P.O. Box 1246, Conifer, CO 80433) and David C. Cook Ministries, Colorado Springs, Colorado.

"Bobo and the Christmas Spirit," by Edith Ballinger Price. If anyone can provide knowledge of first publication source of this old story and whereabouts of author's descendants, please send this information to Joe Wheeler (P.O. Box 1246, Conifer, CO 80433).

"White Wings," by Joseph Leininger Wheeler. Copyright © 2000. Printed by permission of the author.

❄ ❄ ❄

Joseph Leininger Wheeler

INTRODUCTION:
ANNIVERSARY

Whenever I'm interviewed by the media, the one question I'm almost always asked is this: "Tell me, how did this Christmas in My Heart thing happen?" "First of all," I respond, "Joe Wheeler had almost nothing to do with it." Then I take them back—how many years has it been?

It's hard to believe, but ten years have passed since that first collection of Christmas stories was born. Ten years that have dramatically changed the course of my life. I'd guess that most everyone who takes a serious look back into his or her past will stumble upon certain pivotal days and then realize that had those days never been, the course of his or her life would have been far different. Such is the case with me.

"THE SNOW OF CHRISTMAS"

Connie and I had moved to Arnold, Maryland in the summer of 1986, settling on the banks of the shimmering Severn River. From our home, we could hear the sounds of seagulls and great blue herons and watch powerboats and sailboats skimming along the main channel of the river, as well as sculling crews from the U.S. Naval Academy in Annapolis. That fall I began teaching at Columbia Union College in Takoma Park, Maryland. Good years followed, and I fully intended to remain there until retirement, but God had other plans.

The first life-changing day occurred in November 1989. One of my students, an English major, was visiting with us in our home for the weekend. As the winter winds howled outside, we sat inside, enjoying the warmth of a crackling fire in the fireplace. It had been a long, hard week and I was exhausted. What a relief to just sit there in my brown easy chair and dream! But our visitor was not interested in dreaming. She jolted me out of my reverie with a question:

"Dr. Wheeler, have you ever thought of writing a Christmas story?"

I told her—rather unenthusiastically, as I remember it—that I hadn't.

"Well," she retorted, "why don't you?"

I twisted uneasily in my seat, not at all liking the turn the conversation was taking. I decided to pull rank on her and get back to my dreaming, and thus pronounced, in my most exalted manner,

"I will, someday."

But clearly I hadn't realized the mettle of my antagonist. Not at all squelched by her professor's determination to procrastinate, she persisted:

"Why don't you do it tonight? I want to read it and proof each page as you write it."

I almost spit out the coffee I'd been drinking. Who did she think she was, anyway, to try and tell *me* what to do? No bass hooked on a line has ever struggled harder to get off than I did that night. But my visitor, who seemed to take fiendish delight in watching my vain efforts to free myself, kept the line taut. Unfortunately for me, this young woman was a student in my creative writing class. All semester long, I had told her (in no uncertain terms) that come next Monday, or Thursday, she'd better have completed a given writing assignment. No eastern monarch was more impervious to excuses than I—and now she had turned the tables on me!

My last hope was the good Lord: if He would but grant me a wondrous case of writer's block, I could escape her hook. But the Lord ganged up on me too, bringing a promising plot to mind almost instantly. It had to do with a young man who, in the midst of a quarrel with his wife, loses his temper and walks out on his family.

I can see my student through the lens of memory now, sitting there in that chair across the alcove with that unrelenting glint in her eye. She took sadistic delight in marking up each page of text, condescendingly telling me what I needed to do in order to bring it up to snuff. And not until she was fully satisfied did she give up on any of those pages.

And so passed the weekend. *Finally,* she was satisfied. In

fact, she urged me to give copies of "The Snow of Christmas" to students, colleagues, and friends. This proved to be another pivotol point in my career, for the next fall people said, "Well, Joe, you wrote a Christmas story *last* year, what's keeping you from writing one *this* year?" And that's how "The Bells of Christmas Eve" came into being, and the following year, " 'Meditation' in a Minor Key."

A MEMORABLE FIELD TRIP

God never does anything by halves. My second life-changing day occurred about two years after the first one. I had taken a group of creative writing students on a field trip to Review and Herald Publishing Association, Inc., one of the nation's oldest publishers—and Maryland's largest. On this particular day, I left my class with their guide and wandered around a bit on my own. One of the offices I noted was that of Penny Estes Wheeler, Acquisitions Editor. Figuring that with a last name like Wheeler she couldn't be all bad, I decided to get acquainted. I discovered that she was familiar with some writing I had done, mainly in magazines. After some small talk, Penny asked me a leading question:

"Well, what have you written lately?"

I stammered a bit, then answered, "Oh, a couple of Christmas stories."

"Is that all?"

"Yes, but I've been collecting them all my life."

"What kind?"

"Well . . . uh . . . the kind that are Christ-centered rather than Santa Claus-centered."

"Yes?"

"And . . . uh . . . the kind you can't read without crying."

After laughing, she moved in for the kill. "You know, there's a real vacuum in the market for that kind of story. Why don't you put together a collection of your favorite stories and send them to me?"

Since she was astute enough not to tie me to a deadline, I agreed to do it. Then I returned home and proceeded to forget what I had promised.

I can procrastinate with great enthusiasm and this project was no exception. But every once in a while, Penny would call or write me, asking how the manuscript was coming. It wasn't, but I hated to tell her so. Weeks and months—many months—passed, and still I did nothing. But Penny, too, knew how to keep a fishing line taut: she gave me no wiggle room at all. At last I put the manuscript together and mailed it to her, my conscience finally at rest.

Weeks passed, then months. On one never-to-be-forgotten day, the phone rang, and Penny's voice was on the line. These were her words:

"Joe, the committee has cried its way through your manuscript—and we'd like to publish it."

I agreed, and forces were set in motion. Mighty ones. Many a book dies or wilts on the vine because somewhere along the publishing process, something goes awry. Be it cover design or color, interior graphics or illustrations, marketing or manufacturing—so much can go wrong. That nothing *did* go wrong, I owe to two remarkable women: Penny and then-Director of Marketing Susan Harvey. In their strategizing sessions they asked two crucial questions:

"What kind of cover art could be as timeless as the featured stories?" and

"What kind of interior illustrations could be equally timeless?"

Cover-wise, the answer came quickly. The only Christmas artwork that was as timeless as the stories was that done by the studios of Currier and Ives well over a century ago.

As for the inside illustrations, the answer was equally obvious: Only the old-time woodcut was that timeless.

One thing then led to another. We obtained permission to use the earliest generation of Currier and Ives prints and set to work trying to match story lines with the woodcuts. Penny had come up with the title "Christmas in My Heart" a number of years earlier when she had prepared a Christmas anthology for her immediate family. Now she offered it for use with our new book.

When the book came out at last in early autumn of 1992, there was no number on it, for none of us expected there to be another. I turned my full attention to teaching once again, certain that my anthologizing career would begin and end with that one book.

But God perceived my future otherwise. He left nothing to chance, jump-starting me in a direction I would never have chosen on my own.

Our first book sold not only through its first printing but through a second one as well. Penny then called and asked if I'd be willing to put together another anthology. Since we had greatly reduced the size of the first collection and still had many great Christmas stories left, I agreed to do a second book.

This new Christmas in My Heart collection now came with a number. Then came a third, and a fourth. By then

I realized that if we wanted these collections to feature woodcuts that matched the story lines, Connie and I must be willing to spend a great deal of energy, time, and money searching through old illustrated books and magazines to find appropriate illustrations. By the fourth collection, we had pulled it off: most readers assumed the woodcut illustrations originated with their respective stories.

GOD'S MINISTRY, NOT MINE

With each year that passes, it's become ever clearer to me that this ministry of stories is not my own, but God's. I am, at most, a privileged partner. Were that not so, I'd still be teaching full time in the formal classroom rather than writing these words this golden October day from the top of Colorado's Conifer Mountain.

Let me share with you some of the ways I've seen God working in this amazing journey. One of the people I most respect and admire is Dr. James Dobson, president and founder of Focus on the Family. When my first book came out, I sent him a copy, knowing of his love for stories. No response. The same was true with the second. And the third. Then one day I received a phone call from a dear friend at Focus. It began this way, "Joe, are you sitting down?" She went on to say that Dr. Dobson had fallen in love with a story in *Christmas in My Heart 2*, "The Tiny Foot," written by Dr. Frederic Loomis. Would I permit Dr. Dobson to feature that story in his Christmas letter and in his Christmas broadcast? Of course I said yes. Once "The Tiny Foot" was read to tatters in over three million homes and read on the air around the world, and Christmas in My Heart was offered as a Focus premium, I quickly began to lose control of my life. I later became acquainted with Dr. Dobson and discovered what a truly selfless man he is. He's idealistic, caring, and best of all, he cries as easily as I do when he reads a truly sentimental story. Since that time, I have been privileged to partner with Focus on the Family with the Great Stories Remembered anthologies, and Great Stories Classic Books. And beginning in 1998, I tri-partnered with Tyndale House and Focus on the Family to publish the Heart to Heart story anthologies as well as their own editions of Christmas in My Heart. This is their third collection.

Another miracle was the coming into our lives of our agent, Greg Johnson of Alive Communications, Inc. Without him, we could not have made the quantum leap from the paycheck world to a world where we live day to day, trusting God to meet our needs even without a regular paycheck each month.

Then we met Dr. Mark Fretz, then-Senior Religion Editor at Doubleday. He said, in essence, "Joe, your Christmas in My Heart books are available in Christian bookstores, but don't you think they ought to be available in the secular marketplace as well?" And thus was born the Doubleday/Random House hardback Christmas in My Heart series (series title was changed to Christmas in My Soul in 2000).

Meanwhile, the Review and Herald series—where all this started—continued in its original format, unchanged year after year. And here is yet another evidence of God's hand behind the scenes. In that very first collection, I told readers, "If you love these old Christmas stories, let me know, and send me your personal favorites, so that should we ever put out another collection we'll have additional stories from which to choose." They did, and were it not for readers like you continuing to flood our mailbox with your favorite stories, these Christmas collections would have come to an end some time ago. Long ago I vowed, "If I ever get to the point where a new story collection is weaker than its predecessor, it will be time to close the series down." It has never yet happened, for each time I've been convinced that *this is the best one yet!*

THE REST OF THE STORY

It is humbling to look back through these years and see how God has taken these simple little books and made them best-sellers. The variables remain unchanged: an old-time cover, old-time illustrations (mostly woodcuts over a century old) for each story, a heart-warming classic tale, and at the end, one of my own stories. There is one constant: each story must move me deeply. These stories should appeal to your deepest emotions; they should take you somewhere new, make you kinder, more loving, and more empathetic. I believe there is no such thing as a great author, only great stories. Therefore, I do not choose solely on the basis of author name recognition, no matter how eminent, but rather on the basis of the story itself. If a story by a famous author is on my desk alongside one by a totally unknown writer, neither will have the edge: the power of the story alone will be the determining factor.

I have discovered that great stories are great bridges. I know that I can safely give one of these books to my Hindu, Shinto, or Muslim friends without offending them. For I can say, in effect, *You may be a Muslim, and I a Christian, but since both of us want our children to grow up to be loving, kind, appreciative, generous, respectful, honest, altruistic, industrious, imaginative, helpful, and supportive, these stories help bridge the gap between us and allow us to meet on common ground. Then we will realize that in truth we are brothers and sisters, each wanting to make a real difference in this short life we are granted, and each wanting our children to internalize values worth living by.* We don't know how long Christmas in My Heart will continue. But I personally agree with the statement posted in the Focus on the Family Visitor Center: *When people such as you are no longer convicted that they should continue to support this ministry, it will be time to shut our doors, for it will indicate that our work is done.* Thus when people no longer look forward to the next Christmas in My Heart collection, then it will be time to end the series. But the near-fatal head–on collision (with a closing speed of one hundred miles per hour) Connie and I were involved in last February 25 convinces us that God isn't through with us yet. Thus the series continues.

We thank you for all your prayers, encouraging letters, and story submissions down through the years. We will continue to need them as we enter our second decade of Christmas in My Heart. May the good Lord bless and guide you.

THE TENTH COLLECTION

We wanted this anniversary collection to be an extra-special one, both in story plot and in illustration. We hope you feel it's the best one yet.

A number of the writers included are by now old favorites to readers of this series. Grace Livingston Hill appeared once previously ("Forgotten Friend," in book 9). Pearl S. Buck has appeared three times prior to this one ("Stranger, Come Home," "Christmas Day in the Morning," and "Matthew, Mark, Luke, and John," in books 2, 4, and 6, respectively). But Margaret E. Sangster, Jr. has a stranglehold on first place, placing seven times out of ten! (Her previous stories are "The Littlest Orphan and the Christ Baby," "Lonely Tree," "With a Star on Top," "Small Things," "Special Delivery," and "Like a Candle in the Window," in books 2, 3, 5, 6, 8, and 9, respectively.)

In other anthologies I have featured P. J. Platz, Harriet Lummis Smith, Anna Brownell Dunaway, and Harry Harrison Kroll. Appearing for the first time between our covers are Bernadine Beatie, D. T. Doig, Seth Parker, Frank V. McMillan, Adeline Sergeant, Thomas J. Burns, and Edith Ballinger Price.

The write-in story of the year? It is, without question, Seth Parker's "No Man Need Walk Alone."

CODA

I look forward to hearing from you! Please do keep the stories, responses, and suggestions coming—and not just for Christmas stories. I am putting together collections centered around other genres as well. You may reach me by writing to:

Joe L. Wheeler, Ph.D.
c/o Tyndale House Publishers, Inc.
351 Executive Drive
Carol Stream, IL 60188

May the Lord bless and guide the ministry of these stories in your home.

Bernadine Beatie

THE SHEAF
OF GRAIN

It was a Christmas story the old man told—but it
was a Christmas story with an unhappy ending.
*   If only—*

*J*t was Christmas Eve. Young Mike sat at the window of his home, looking down the highway to the west. He could just see the lights of Grandpa's filling station glimmering through the swirling snow. In front of every house on each side of the highway there stood a tall pole to which a sheaf of grain had been attached.

"Ma," Young Mike called, "may I go stay with Grandpa?"

"You just want to hear your grandpa's Christmas story again," Ma said, coming to stand beside Mike. "Sometimes I think we hang those sheaves of grain more to please your grandpa than for any other reason."

"No," said Mike, "for the birds and for Olaf."

"Humph!" Ma said. "Everybody but your grandpa knows Olaf has been dead these many years. Nobody could have lived through that storm."

Mike supposed Ma was right, but it was too bad. Grandpa wanted a better ending for his Christmas story—a happy one. So did Mike.

"Well, run along," Ma said. "But you and your grandpa close up and be home by ten." Mike reached the filling station just as a large car pulled into the drive. A tall man slid from beneath the wheel. He wore a trim-looking dark-blue uniform and a cap with a visor that was covered with gold braid. He looked larger than life, somehow, outlined against the dark snow-swept prairie. Mike's eyes bulged when he heard his grandfather call the man "Captain." Mike had never seen a sea captain before.

"Tell me," the stranger asked, "why are sheaves of grain hanging before all the houses?"

Old Mike perked up. "Do you have time to hear a story?"

"There is always time for a story," said the man from the sea.

"Come inside," Grandpa said, "where it's warm."

The stranger shook his head when Grandpa offered him a chair near the small hissing stove. Instead, he pulled his cap low over his eyes and sat in a shadowy corner of the small room. Grandpa took his regular place beside the stove, and Mike sat beside him, hoping no customers would come and disturb the telling of the story.

"Once, many years ago," Grandpa started, "a rancher and his wife here were very fond of children. Years passed, and when no children came to bless their home, they started caring for homeless boys who came their way. And there were many of them, for those were the days of the Great Depression, when hunger stalked the land.

"First one boy drifted in, and then another, until every room of the rancher's home was filled with homeless boys. They were a rough lot, those lads, rough and wild. The rancher was always getting them out of scrapes at school or in town. Many folks around said he was just raising them for the jailhouse. Maybe he was— they were a wild bunch all right!

"Then, one spring day, a different kind of lad drifted in. He was tall, with hair the color of sun-ripened wheat, and he gave his name as Olaf Jensen. He came from a land far across the sea, and he was as strong as a winter storm. Yet, there was something strangely gentle and kind about him. Flowers he planted bloomed more quickly than others, birds sang when he was near, and the orneriest critter on the ranch would settle down at the sound of Olaf's voice."

Young Mike looked up, knowing Grandpa would pause at this point—he always did. And Young Mike knew too that there would be a faraway look in Old Mike's eyes, almost as though he were hearing Olaf's voice.

"Yes?" the tall stranger prompted softly.

"The boys did not like Olaf," Grandpa continued. "He was different from them. 'Yah,' he said, instead of 'yes,' and sometimes he spoke in a strange foreign tongue. They felt, too, that the old rancher and his wife had a feeling for Olaf that they didn't have for them, and thus they grew jealous. When the rancher and his wife were not around, the boys tormented Olaf with every meanness they could think of. The ringleader was a boy named Mike.

"This grieved Olaf, who looked on every living thing with love."

Young Mike hitched his chair a little closer to the stove, struck with wonder that Grandpa had once been the young Mike of the story—wild and rough.

"Why didn't this Olaf fight back?" the stranger spoke from the shadows.

"One day he did. One Christmas Eve—snowy and cold—very much like today. Olaf had attached a sheaf of grain to a pole and stuck it in the ground fifty yards from the house.

" 'For the birds,' Olaf said. 'It is a custom in the country of my people.' The boys laughed at him, pulled down the pole, and scattered the grain. Olaf replaced the grain and the pole time after time. Finally, the boys

4

tired of the sport and left the pole standing. Later, however, Mike saw a bird fluttering around the grain, took a slingshot and killed it. Olaf saw. He ran forward, touched the bird with gentle fingers, then he turned on Mike, his eyes flashing blue fire. He threw Mike to the ground and fell on him.

"The other boys, shocked by the fury of Olaf's rage, pulled at him.

" 'Stop! You'll kill him!' one of the boys cried.

"The madness and anger gradually left Olaf's face, and was replaced by a deep sadness. 'I go now,' he said softly. 'I bring only unhappiness to this place. My heart is sick. When it heals, perhaps I will return.' Olaf buttoned his jacket around his neck and disappeared into the swirling snow.

"The boys were frightened as the storm developed into a blizzard. It was twenty miles to the nearest town. Olaf would surely die! They went to the rancher and told him.

"The rancher stood very straight and looked at them. 'Where have I failed you, my sons?' he asked sadly. And he saddled a horse and rode out into the storm, searching for Olaf.

"Darkness fell, and he did not return. The boys saddled horses and formed a line to search, calling to each other so that none would get lost in the storm. After many hours, they found the old rancher, fallen from his horse and half-buried in the snow. They wrapped him in their coats and carried him to a line shack that was used during roundup time. But the old man was burning up with fever; without medicine and warm food death was certain.

"The boys drew lots to see who would go for help. It fell to Mike. He rode out, pulling his cap down against the blinding snow. Soon he was lost in a white world of darkness. But he rode on, hoping his horse would take him home. Then his horse shied at an unknown sound, and Mike was thrown to the ground. He grabbed for the reins, but his horse was gone. Mike stood up then stumbled on. He prayed—this Mike who had never prayed before prayed for strength to find help for his friends and for the old rancher who had befriended them all.

"But after a long time, he knew his strength was gone. He stumbled and fell. He could go no farther. Then his hands closed on something—upon a pole standing above the snow. Attached to the top was a sheaf of grain. Olaf's pole! And Olaf's pole saved the life of the old rancher, for Mike found the ranch house and help was sent."

"What happened to those other boys?" the stranger asked.

Grandpa seemed lost in dreams, so Young Mike took up the story. "They changed after that. They settled down and tried to be good sons to the old rancher. Most of them are still living close by, and many of their sons and daughters, too."

"That's the reason," Grandpa finished up, "for the sheaves of grain."

"So no trace was ever found of Olaf?" the stranger asked.

"No," Young Mike said. "That's the part of the story I don't like—the ending."

The stranger chuckled softly. "How should it end?"

"Olaf should come back!" Young Mike said. "He should come back and learn that he did not bring unhappiness after all; that, because of him, the boys gave up their wild ways!" Mike sighed. "Christmas stories should have happy endings."

The stranger stood. He seemed to fill the room as he swept the cap from his head. His hair was snow white, but the unshaded light hanging from the ceiling turned it the color of sun-ripened wheat.

Young Mike's eyes were wide as saucers, and the only sound in the room was the soft hissing of the stove.

Then Grandpa moved forward. His face was like an answered dream as he grasped the sea captain's extended hand. "Olaf—*Olaf!*" Grandpa whispered.

Very softly, Young Mike crept from the room. It seemed fitting, somehow, that the two old men should finish the telling of the story alone. But he smiled and hugged the happy ending to his heart.

Bernadine Beatie

Bernadine Beatie wrote for inspirational journals in the mid-twentieth century.

D. J. Doig

A PRECIOUS MEMORY

It was Christmas again, but not Christmas as it once was, before Timmy. . . . Now there was a coldness between Mom and Dad. But the Family Cake was the last straw—or might it be the last hope? This recent Christmas story is, without question, one of the great ones.

I'm not sure who invented the Family Cake. My mother called it that, and for all I know it might have been her own idea. For as long as I can remember it has always been a part of Christmas.

Mom was a great one for making cakes and decorating them to suit the occasion—birthdays, anniversaries, weddings, Thanksgivings, even the Fourth of July.

But the Family Cake for Christmas was always the special one. It appeared in its full glory at supper on Christmas Eve, a prelude to all the surprises, mysteries, and excitement that were to come. The best thing about it was that Mom had carefully put all our names on it in different-colored icing.

There were five of us altogether, and each wedge of cake bore one name. Bob and Ruth were the names of Mom and Dad. Then there was Bess—that was I—the eldest. Then Matthew, five years younger; and finally little Timmy, who was the youngest. Each section had its candle, and a tiny Santa Claus stood in the middle, its feet stuck in the icing.

I had the honor, being the eldest child, of lighting the candles and carrying the cake in for dessert. There was always a loud cheer when I brought it in.

I can still see little Timmy in his high chair, his fingers clenched with excitement, his eyes glistening in the candlelight. He would gaze in wonder at the cake, the Christmas tree, the decorations. When Mom cut the cake, Timmy had to have his name pointed out so that he was sure his piece was the right one. Then he would clap his hands and laugh with joy.

My father would joke all through the meal and tell

Mom how pretty she looked, and how lucky she was to have such a splendid family. It was a happy time.

Then one year Mom didn't make the Family Cake. That was the Christmas when Timmy wasn't there any more.

I was twelve when it happened. March was busy on the farm, with so many calves being born and all the lambing as well. Some of Dad's calves got scour, a difficult ailment to cure, and he seldom had a minute to himself.

One afternoon, Mom had to go into town for an appointment with the doctor, and Mrs. Harris, our part-time help, was ill. Matthew and I were in school so it fell to Dad to look after Timmy for two or three hours.

There was nothing special about that, for we were all used to taking turns caring for Timmy. Things seemed to be quiet on the farm that day, and Dad promised to take Timmy fishing for a couple of hours until Mom got back. The stream nearby flowed into an old mill pond, and it was often possible to find trout there.

They were just setting off when one of the farmhands came to report trouble with a newborn calf. Dad took Timmy with him to the shed where the calf and its mother were lying. Dad told Timmy to sit down on a bale of hay and wait.

While the business of working on the calf went on, it took the men a while to realize that Timmy was no longer there. Dad abandoned the calf at once and looked everywhere—in the house, in the tractor shed, and all over the barns. Soon everybody on the farm, as well as the neighbors, had joined in the search. Minutes dragged on into an hour and an hour into two hours.

It was Mrs. Harris's husband who found Timmy in the mill pond. He had wandered quietly down to the stream to look for fish. Nobody could tell how it had happened. We only knew when he was taken out it was too late.

❄ ❄ ❄

After that, things could never be the same. All through that spring and summer we lived our lives and did the ordinary tasks. And we hid our grief as best we could when we weren't alone.

Dad was quieter now, and Mom went around with a brooding look on her face. She often spoke to Dad in a hard tone I hadn't heard before. Although I was only twelve, I knew something more than our loss was driving them apart.

I sensed that she blamed Dad for what had happened to Timmy. In her mind it had to be somebody's fault. Perhaps hers for not being there.

During all that time I never saw her cry, but there were times when she seemed like a statue or like somebody who was sleepwalking. Never once did she mention Timmy.

The months passed. Time began its work of healing, but the old, warm feeling of being a united family was no more. And yet my mother was even more attentive than before toward Matthew and me, anxiously watchful and protective. But between her and my father there remained a gulf—a distance which showed, not in silence, but in the lack of companionship and a certain wariness in their conversation.

Once, when they thought I had gone out of the house, I heard Dad say, "If that's how you feel, I could go and stay with Charles in Ontario."

I didn't think at the time that it meant anything more than a visit to an uncle, who was also a farmer, in Canada. Charles was Dad's brother, and I could barely remember the tall, wide-shouldered man who had once come here to see us.

But as the weeks passed and I sometimes caught the word *Canada* just before they broke off a conversation, I began to be afraid. Maybe Dad wasn't going there just for a visit.

Matthew, who was barely seven years old, wasn't aware of my fears or what caused them. He was the one who talked about Timmy, and he often talked to me about the things Timmy had said or done. He seemed to know I was the one who would really listen.

❅ ❅ ❅

Harvest time came, and with it a golden spell of sun and ripeness. The early September days with their mellow plenty made me feel that the happy, close-knit days would come back again. My mother was busier than I had ever seen her. She never seemed to be still, and in October she and Mrs. Harris set about their usual task of brightening the house for the approach of Christmas.

They painted the kitchen and all the bedrooms. It was a bustling time, and any visitor would have thought that ours was a cheerful home that housed a happy family.

I knew, though, that it was all on the surface, and lurking beneath was a shadow that we couldn't chase away. Dad sometimes tried to bring back the old fun and banter. Matthew and I would always respond, but it would only be when Mom wasn't around.

Once, when the cleaning was going on, I saw Mrs. Harris stop outside the room that had been Timmy's. "Do you want me to start on this one?" she quietly asked my mother.

"No. We'll leave that for now," Mom replied very quickly.

In time, of course, December came around. There was no question that we wouldn't celebrate Christmas the way we always had.

A week before Christmas Day, Dad cut a spruce tree from the woods and soon all the baubles and lights were glittering in the corner of the living room. The other decorations went up one by one—festoons, the bright holly, and the sparkling tinsel. We wrapped our presents as usual and hid them until it was time to put them under the tree. The snow came in short, powdery showers, just enough to bring its extra magic to the bare trees and hedges.

It was just two days before Christmas Eve when I asked, "Have you made the Family Cake yet, Mom?"

She stopped what she was doing, and again I saw the sad, defeated look come into her eyes. "No, Bess. There's so much to do, and I don't think I'll have time. Maybe I'll make a special cake for New Year's Eve."

It was a bitter disappointment, like a broken promise, or as if something warm that had been a part of our lives no longer bound us all together.

I opened my mouth to protest, but then I realized she wasn't really telling me the truth. All the constraint between my mother and father, all the unnatural silences and the strange, secret discord suddenly swelled in my throat, and I could contain my fears no longer.

"Mom—is Dad going away to live in Canada?"

That startled her, and she replied without looking directly at me. "We haven't decided anything yet. But your Dad hasn't seen Uncle Charles for a very long time, and a change might do him good. It's been a hard year for him—and for us all."

Again, I was aware of hearing only half of the truth. I felt all the sure and safe things in our lives were slipping away. Tears filled my eyes, but I fought them back. "Why can't we all be happy again?" I cried, and turned away without waiting for an answer.

❅ ❅ ❅

I didn't tell Matthew what I had found out about Canada. I suppose I still hoped it wouldn't happen. But I did tell him there was to be no Family Cake. He looked at me with round, disbelieving eyes.

"But, there's *always* been a Family Cake, Bess! It's the one where we all have our own special piece with our name and a candle on it. You know!"

I put my arm around him and made myself sound cheerful. "Never mind. Maybe I'll think up another surprise."

As I spoke, I suddenly knew what I was going to do. "I tell you what! If Mom can't make a Family Cake, we'll make it ourselves."

"Are you sure you know how?" he said, doubt in his voice. "Suppose Mom won't let us?"

By now I was gripped with a firm resolve. "I've watched her making it before and I think I can do it. We'll keep it secret until Christmas Eve. Mrs. Harris will help us, and we can take all the things to her house and do it there."

That was how we spent the next two days, in conspiracy and excitement—Mrs. Harris enjoying the plot, covering up our absences from the house.

I'll admit that I needed more help with the preparation than I had thought, but I managed to do all the icing part myself, although it wasn't as neat and pretty as it would have been with Mom's expert touch.

Matthew watched me do it, leaning over Mrs. Harris's kitchen table with breathless concentration. "It's got to be like it always is," he said constantly. "Timmy's piece has got to be there too. It's his cake as well as ours, and his name has to be in blue."

Finally it was finished. We had bought the ingredients, and candles, and the funny little Santa Claus out of our allowances and put a pink and green ribbon around the cake.

Smuggling it into our house wasn't easy, but in the end the cake was brought home after dark on Christmas Eve and safely hidden in a cupboard on the porch.

❄ ❄ ❄

Christmas Eve was the kind of day that happens in almost every home—friends bringing presents, Mom or Dad making hurried visits to the store for things that had almost been forgotten, and a general trend toward the kitchen, where my mother ruled with her usual grace. All that was missing was that mysterious something that had wielded its magic in other years. I could tell it was gone and I didn't know any way of bringing it back.

Dad tried to make Christmas seem as much fun as it ever was. He poured punch for us all and teased Matthew about hanging his stocking too low on the mantel. Even Mom smiled once or twice, and for a moment the family feeling came alive again.

It didn't last long. I caught Dad watching Mom with that lost look, knowing that he was wishing she would join in.

When supper was served, Matthew and I were so keyed up we could hardly eat a thing. We had agreed that as soon as the main course was over, I would make an excuse and go out to the porch cupboard for the cake. I had matches ready to light the candles. My heart was beating fast as I slipped out to the back.

It seemed to take ages to get the five candles lit, but at length I was ready. It was a smaller cake than the one Mom usually made, and the names on it were a bit blotchy, but it looked brave with its colors and candles. I was proud of it.

They were still sitting there when I carried it in and set it on the center of the table. Nobody spoke at first, but Matthew's face wore a triumphant grin.

Dad flashed a quick look at Mom, and said, "Well, where did that come from? I thought the Family Cake had gotten lost this year."

I put my arm around Matthew and laughed with the pleasure of seeing our plan succeed. "It's our surprise. Mom was so busy we thought we would do it ourselves—well, nearly by ourselves."

Mom said nothing. Her face had gone quite pale and she sat looking down at the cake with all the names on it. When she spoke her voice was hoarse and tight. "You shouldn't have done that. I told you there would be no cake. It doesn't mean the same anymore."

Matthew's smile vanished. I felt all the love and brightness fade into the hopeless feeling I knew so well. My despair was followed by a hot wave of anger.

"I don't understand!" I burst out. "It's a *Family* Cake! We're still a family, aren't we?"

I was looking straight at my mother, and I couldn't stop the words tumbling out. "Is it because Timmy's name is on it? Do we have to leave him out of everything because he isn't here? Wherever he is, he would want it like this. He loved Christmas and the Family Cake. And he loved us, too. It's not fair to shut him out!"

I sat down, nervous and drained. It was Dad who spoke gently then to Mother. "Bess is right, Ruth. We have to accept things as they are, otherwise we'll destroy all we've got left."

Suddenly, it was like a dam breaking. Tears began to spill over my mother's cheeks—something I hadn't seen during all the long months since March. She pushed back her chair and hurried out of the room.

Dad followed her. Matthew and I were left alone, silent and shaken, looking at the festive table with the remains of the meal and the lopsided cake. Now it looked pathetic.

❄ ❄ ❄

It seemed a long time, but after a bit they came back again, Mom and Dad. They stood very close, with Dad's arm around Mom's waist. Her tears were gone, her face flushed, and now she looked calm and somehow beautiful.

She came to me and kissed me. "I'm sorry, Bess," she said, simply.

After that Mom sat down and carefully cut the sections of the cake. Then she served each piece until there was only Timmy's portion, alone on the dish.

For me it was as if a storm had passed, leaving flowers limp but grateful for the rain. There was a new light in Dad's eyes, and I couldn't restrain myself from asking the question that was still in the front of my mind.

"Are you really going away to Canada, Dad?" I asked.

He smiled and shook his head. "Maybe next year when I find someone to look after the farm, we'll all go there for a vacation."

As we talked I heard a sound from outside, faint above the wailing wind.

"It's the carol singers!" Matthew shouted excitedly. "They're here!"

"Go and bring them in, Matthew," Dad said, "and we'll make some hot drinks for them."

There were seven singers, all young people we knew. They were glad to come inside out of the cold. After the cocoa was finished, they ranged themselves around our table and sang my favorite Christmas hymn.

It sounded especially beautiful because in spite of all

the trouble we had passed through, we were a family again. I saw that Mom and Dad were holding hands and their eyes often met, something I hadn't seen in a long time.

And in the center of the table, on the untouched piece of cake, Timmy's little candle burned bravely on like a tiny beacon of faith.

David T. Doig

David T. Doig was a native of Scotland and died there in 1990. He was an extremely prolific writer, and his stories have been published all around the world.

P. J. Platz

LIGHTS OF
THE SEASON

Here she was, a pregnant woman, standing on a teetering ladder, trying to string 2,500 Christmas lights on the tree in her front yard. Was she crazy?

And now this—none of them worked! And that Mr. McElroy next door! Just the thought of him infuriated her.

A gust of wind caught the hem of Madeline's wool scarf and whipped it across her face, startling her. She jerked involuntarily, felt the ladder sway beneath her, and clutched in terror at the top branches of the spruce.

"Mommy! Are you hugging the tree?" Jenny called from near the house, her little five-year-old voice nearly whisked away by the wind.

Madeline nodded jerkily, her eyes wide, her heart pounding. *I am,* she thought; *that's precisely what I'm doing. I'm a pregnant woman teetering on a ladder in the middle of a snowstorm, hugging the top of a twelve-foot tree. If old man McElroy saw me he'd call the men in the white suits to come and take me away.*

Her eyes moved automatically to the dark, looming house next door. Was that a face at the downstairs window? Was that old grumpy hermit spying on her again?

She shifted her weight just a little and felt a sharp branch poking at her belly. *Hello baby. Merry Christmas.*

"Wait till I tell Daddy you hugged the tree," Jenny giggled, her voice closer now.

Madeline risked a glance downward, saw a dear little figure encased in a thick padding of a red snowsuit, pink nose, pink cheeks, and bright blue eyes turned upward. "Not so close, honey," her voice quavered.

Jenny backed away obediently. "Can we plug in the lights yet?"

Madeline's fingers tightened around the string of lights clutched in her right hand. "Not yet, Jenny. It's a little too windy to get them all up today." She moved boot-heavy feet cautiously down the rungs until she was standing in the snowdrifts at the base of the tree, her knees shaking. "Maybe tomorrow."

Jenny looked up at her and smiled a very adult, very understanding smile that made Madeline feel guilty. How many days had she climbed this ladder, tried to string the lights on this tree, and finally ended with an apologetic "maybe tomorrow"?

"It's okay, Mommy," Jenny said. "We don't have to put the lights up this year."

Madeline forced a smile past the catch in her throat. They *did* have to put the lights up this year, and they had to make chocolate bars and string garland and hang the mistletoe and do everything they normally did for Christmas, because there was one huge thing that was glaringly abnormal about this year—Robert wouldn't be here.

"We'll get the lights up, Jenny," she said stubbornly, careful not to promise, just in case.

Later, rinsing vegetables for supper at the sink, Madeline's eyes lifted to gaze out at the driving snow. *Wonderful,* she thought. *The snowiest Christmas ever. Bah humbug.*

She could barely see old Mr. McElroy's house across the side yard, a black hole in their neighborhood of warmly lit houses. As usual, only one light burned in a downstairs window.

"Maybe he only has one lamp," Robert had remarked once in jest, but after three years of staring at that dark, lifeless house, the joke had lost its humor. Never once had they seen light behind another window; never once had they seen a single visitor approach the shrub-shrouded front door. The old man's ɔne and only concession to this month of holidays was a single string of garish green lights that outlined that downstairs window once a year for a few hours on Christmas Eve. He turned them on at sunset, then off at midnight. The people who sold them the house said it was the last Christmas decoration Mrs. McElroy had put up before her death ten years before, and the story was almost sad enough to make Madeline forgive the old man for his miserable temperament—almost, but not quite.

The day they'd moved in Mr. McElroy stood on his front porch with his arms folded across his chest, glaring at his new neighbors. And then Jenny—two years old then and innocently gregarious—had toddled over to lisp a childish, trusting greeting. He'd simply muttered under his breath and retreated into his house, slamming the door behind him. The only words Madeline had ever heard him speak were a stern warning that first week to keep Jenny—"that child," he'd called her—out of his flower beds. His gruff voice had made Jenny cry, Madeline remembered, and she'd harbored a secret desire ever since to steal over in the dead of night and mow his precious flower beds down to the ground.

The timer on the stove rasped angrily, jarring her out of her reverie.

"Cookies!" Jenny cried happily from where she sat at the kitchen table. "Are those the ones for Mr. McElroy?"

Madeline hurried to the oven and pulled out a tray of fat, puffy Santa Clauses. "That's right, honey. After they cool you can decorate them, okay?"

She was having dark thoughts about making black

icing when Jenny said, "I hope Mr. McElroy likes Santa Claus cookies."

Madeline sighed, humbled by her child's generous spirit. "Well, we've put a box on his front step every Christmas for three years, and he hasn't sent them back yet. He must like them." She pressed a hand to the small of her aching back and wondered, as she did every year, why she continued to bake cookies for a miserable old man who hadn't said a kind word to any of them in over three years.

"Mommy?"

"Hmm?"

"Is tonight the night Daddy's calling?"

"Tomorrow night, honey. Christmas Eve."

Jenny's sigh was so dramatically plaintive that it made Madeline smile. She turned to look at where her daughter sat at the kitchen table, a stubby, oversized pencil clutched tightly in her small, pudgy hand.

"Another letter to Santa, honey?"

Jenny nodded without looking up from the laborious, jerky tracks the pencil was making on the paper. Little lips were folded in on one another, and tiny pale brows were knit in a concentration so fierce that it tugged at Madeline's heartstrings, making her want to weep.

Of course, everything made her want to weep these days. *Hormones on the rampage,* she thought, blinking rapidly; *courtesy of being pregnant and complicated by an absentee husband. Which is what you get for falling in love with a career Navy man,* she berated herself.

"I'm asking Santa to bring Daddy home for Christmas," Jenny was saying. "That's all I want."

Madeline turned rapidly back to the sink and scowled

down at the carrot she was peeling. "Santa can't do that, honey. Daddy has to stay on his ship just a little longer before he gets a vacation. Remember when Daddy and I explained about Christmas being a little late this year?"

"Christmas isn't going to be late, Mommy. Daddy is."

Madeline smiled. "You're absolutely right, Jenny. And that means we'll have two Christmases. One with just you and me, and another in three weeks when Daddy comes home."

Jenny put her little chin in her palm and pursed her lips thoughtfully. "Maybe Daddy can put the lights on the tree in the front yard when he comes home."

Madeline frowned. "I think I can get the lights up tomorrow, honey."

By late afternoon the next day Madeline eased down the ladder and looked up at the tree with an exhausted smile of supreme contentment. *Anyone who doesn't think this is a season of miracles should come take a look at this tree,* she thought, grinning fiercely at the fifty strings of lights draped around the spruce. The black cord stuck out from the branches like an arthritic snake, and she knew when she plugged it in that some lights would be jammed together in one spot while another was completely bare—but the lights were up there, thank the good Lord.

She caught a glimpse of Mr. McElroy's cold face watching her from his downstairs window. *You didn't think I could do it, did you, you old stinker?* she thought, knowing he'd been watching the process for days, probably anticipating her failure with a mean-spirited glee. "Well, take a look at this, Mr. McElroy," she hissed triumphantly under her breath, jamming the plug into the extension cord.

Nothing happened.

Madeline stood there in the dusky light, gaping at the tree in disbelief, pulling the plug out, then jamming it back in, over and over again.

Check the lights before you string them. If one bulb's gone, none of them will light, Maddie.

Madeline started shaking her head, and couldn't seem to stop. How many times had Robert told her that? And still she'd forgotten. She hadn't checked the lights. She gazed up at the 2,500 absolutely black bulbs in complete dismay, pressing her lips together hard so she wouldn't burst into tears.

Suddenly a rectangle of green blinked on in Mr. McElroy's window. *My lights work and yours don't,* they seemed to say, and Madeline thought she might joyfully throttle the nasty old man at that moment.

Mr. McElroy's green lights mocked her as they backed out of the driveway later, past the dark triangle of their own spruce on their way to church. She stopped the car briefly in front of McElroy's, and watched with a bittersweet expression as Jenny darted up the front walk with a brightly colored tin of decorated Santa Claus cookies, delivering a gift of love to a man who didn't know the meaning of the word.

Jenny placed the tin on the porch, rang the bell, then hurried back to the car, giggling with the sheer joy of giving.

It's the children who are really Santa Claus, Madeline thought, leaning over to buckle Jenny's seatbelt, breathing in the damp, child-sweet smell of her. *As long as we let them be children, giving itself is the gift. But then one day we decide they're too old to believe in the nonsense of some benevolent legend who gives and gives without ever expecting anything in return. That's when we teach them the awful truth about the bartering world of adults, about exchanging gifts, not giving them. That's the day children grow up, and Santa Claus dies.*

It was snowing again when they came out of church, and the sidewalk was drifted with waves of sparkling white that lapped at the tops of their boots. Madeline drove home slowly, past brightly lit homes and trees festooned with lights, almost dreading the sight of their own dark yard.

She took the last turn, her eyes deliberately fixed on the road.

"Mommy!" Jenny cried softly. "Look! Look at our tree!"

Madeline raised her eyes, blinked, then stared with dumbstruck wonder at the pyramid of glorious golden lights winding through the sparkling, snow-covered boughs of their front-yard spruce. "Oh my," she murmured, turning slowly into the drive and turning off the ignition, barely noticing when Jenny scrambled out and slogged through the drifts toward the tree.

Robert, she thought, her heart leaping in her chest. Robert was home. But no, that was impossible. Robert was somewhere in the middle of the dark, endless Pacific. He'd called from the ship just before they'd left for church, his normally strong voice thick with emotion and regret.

Did I leave the extension cord plugged in? she wondered, getting out of the car and pushing through the snow, her gaze fastened on the miracle of the tree that had fixed its own lights. Maybe there wasn't a burned-out bulb after all; maybe they just had to warm up or something. . . .

She smiled at the picture of little Jenny standing at the base of that brightly lit tree, arms stretched up and out as if to embrace the wonder of it. The placement of lights was just as erratic as she'd thought it might be—entire branches were bare and dark, while others seemed weighted down with a cluster of lights, as if someone had dropped a handful of golden nuggets on the boughs. It was an inelegant decorating job, she thought, grinning happily; almost a comical sight, in fact, especially with that single green bulb near the top . . .

Her eyes widened as her mouth dropped open, and then her gaze shifted abruptly across the yard to Mr. McElroy's downstairs window, where the rectangle of green lights no longer shone. . . . *If one bulb's gone, none of them will light, Maddie. . . .*

She jumped when a little hand slipped into hers. "Do you think Santa did it, Mommy?" Jenny whispered, awestruck.

Madeline looked down slowly, her eyes catching the ghostly remnants of large footprints that led across the side yard to old Mr. McElroy's property. They were filling in rapidly with blowing snow. Another few moments and she might never have seen them at all.

"Maybe so, honey," she whispered back, her gaze lifting from the disappearing prints to the very top of their own tree, where a single green bulb glowed in garish contrast to its golden fellows, the brightest light of all.

P. J. Platz

P. J. Platz is the pen name of successful mother/daughter writing team Patricia and Traci Lambrecht. The Lambrechts live in Chisago City, Minnesota. They are prolific writers of short stories as well as movie scripts, and their work shows up in many women's and family magazines.

Harry Harrison Kroll

GOOD WILL
TOWARD MEN

*Dave liked his teaching job—but the Westbrooks,
especially Simon, made his life miserable. And now,
the final blow: a legal warrant for cutting a Christmas
tree on the Westbrook property! Good will toward
men, indeed!*

*T*he Westbrooks were a disagreeable, grasping lot, Dave Conley was thinking, as he crunched through the snow toward the tree. He was a tall, well-knit young man, with a strong face, fine gray-blue eyes, and a chin turned with resolution, mixed with tenderness. He was garbed in old hunting clothes, with high-laced boots. Reaching the holly tree, he examined it from every angle.

"It's just the thing" he said, half aloud. "But I'd better be sure it's off the Westbrook land." He was familiar with the land lines and fences; after some search he saw ax marks in a big poplar near by—three chips and a cross.

That's the line, he thought. In a moment he fell to work, and soon had the tree down. He trimmed it with considerable care, chopped off the base evenly and made ready to drag it down to the wagon waiting at the foot of the hill. He took only a few minutes to drag the tree down. He left it on a rock ledge and drove the wagon to a point where he could gently roll the tree on. He was ready to take it to the schoolhouse, where tomorrow the pupils would put it up and decorate it, making ready for the big event of the Yule tree.

Dave Conley returned to his earlier thinking. He would use huge, laughing, grasping Simon Westbrook for Santa as usual. Simon Westbrook had been Santa now for six or seven years—or was it eight? At any rate, Simon was fat, he had a hearty laugh, and if ever anybody got pleasure out of playing a part, it was Simon playing big, generous Santa Claus. Once Dave had a suspicion that it was because Simon could give away many presents without the necessity of having to put out any money for

them; but as that was rather unkind he didn't harbor the
conviction for long.

Dave Conley had gone away to college, come back
home, and the school board had given him, the past
autumn, a place to teach. The Westbrook clan fought
him tooth and nail. They knew a thousand ways to
annoy the teacher, and at times young Dave thought
that the Westbrook tribe used the whole thousand, plus
a few extra combinations for bad measure. They talked
about him; they said the scholars got into fights on the
grounds and to and from school; they disapproved of
the long recesses. Sometimes Dave did forget and go
overtime a few moments when the play was full of fun.

They magnified every little failing, and overlooked
entirely the fact that Dave Conley had the school in
splendid enthusiasm, with plenty of hard work during
study hours. Best of all, his scholars loved him. Even
one or two of the Westbrook girls and boys secretly
loved Dave. They dared not admit that at home, of
course.

Dave hauled the tree on down to the schoolhouse
where he unloaded it. He then drove the team on to his
boarding place, at Ham Ricks, where he put it up. He
had been home perhaps an hour when Squire Leverage,
chairman of the school board, drove up to the gate in
the wintry sunlight and called.

"Hey, 'fessor!"

Dave went out to the gate. "Come in, Uncle Jesse."

"Nope, got to be riding. I dropped by to tell you I
won't be able to help with the tree—called away on
sickness; so I'm just going to turn all my official jobs
over to you. You see about getting the Santa, and Mis'

Laws has the red suit up at her house. I been thinking about Sim Westbrook. He's awful good at the job, but them Westbrooks haven't done a thing all fall but make trouble, so I'd made up my mind not to let them come in and run the show. So you get up Santa—I'll just leave it to you. If I get back in time I hope to come to the tree. So long, and good luck. Hope you have a grand time."

"Thanks, Squire—we shall."

Squire Leverage drove away. He had been gone less than five minutes when Morris Jones, the constable, came up on horseback. Dave turned at the call, thinking, whimsically, that it was a busy day for him.

"Hello, Mr. Jones. 'Light and come in."

"Thankee, Dave—I got a little business here with you. Some papers." He was hesitant, as he fumbled in his pockets.

"Papers?" said Dave, in surprise.

"Warrant. Swore out in Squire Jake Westbrook's co't. I didn't much want to serve it, but duty is duty—you know how them things is, 'fessor."

The young man stood there a bit stupefied. "Warrant!" he repeated, in a tight voice. "For *what?*"

The constable produced the legal paper, and read the charge. "For willfully stealing a tree off Simon and Clay Westbrook's land."

"Why—why—" gasped Dave. "Tree! You mean, that Christmas tree? Why, my goodness, they must have broken some necks to get this warrant sworn out, for it's only been two hours since I cut the tree. Besides, it's not from their land. I looked carefully for the lines."

"I'm skeered," said Jones, doubtfully, "that you made

some kind of a mistake, 'fessor, for the tree shore did come off the Westbrook land. I rode by the place to make sure where it happened, and everything. He was standing behind another tree, no piece at all off, and he seen you cutting it, him and another feller. I know you didn't mean no harm, 'fessor, but that's the way it is, and I'm sort of skeered that it may mess you up right smart, if they keep pushing it. You know what sort of folks they are—stubborn, hard-headed, and once they've put their mean hands to the plow, they bust out the middle or bust up the plow."

"I know," said Dave Conley, for the first time with a hint of bitterness. "Well, I reckon there's nothing I can do about it but face it out. I dread it, though—on account of the school. I should have had sense enough to make sure."

"If it had happened on this side the line, you could get the case in Jedge Leverage's co't. He'd throw it out, and throw out Simon Westbrook, too. But since it's going to go through the Westbrook hands in trial, it's going to be a right smart mess. Most folks, 'fessor, will take your side. Don't worry."

"All the same, the trial is bound to react against the school."

"Y-yes, that's right. To some extent. But fight it out. Don't let 'em put anything over on you. Here's the bond. Sign it. Get somebody to go on with you, or you can give me a signed check for the amount of bond to appear two weeks from now before Squire Jake Westbrook."

Dave signed the papers, wrote the check, and the constable turned and went back as he had come.

The whole disagreeable affair took the flavor out of the Christmas season for young Dave Conley. "Peace on earth, good will toward men"—what irony it was! The fact that the incident was merely technical guilt did not matter. He should have taken more care. To that extent he certainly was blameworthy. Nor was it of any moment that the tree itself was worth little or nothing. He had taken something off somebody's property, without permission. Perhaps the tree, cut and trimmed and taken to the city, would have fetched two dollars. The ugliness of a small matter magnified into a big one was that which annoyed Dave.

While the scholars put up the tree in the schoolhouse, and the big girls decorated it beautifully with colored papers and glass ornaments, Dave Conley watched with a sense of moroseness. All the Yuletide sweetness was gone from him.

Meanwhile, of course, in the Westbrook camp was a good amount of gratification. Simon Westbrook, throwing out his barrel chest, would smite himself heroically, and laugh in that vast manner he had: "I ketched the 'fessor on his blind side that time, and socked him one that'll hold him a spell!" Then his face hardened. His eyes glinted. "He thinks he's some pumpkins—go off and take on a jag of book-l'arning, then come back and gooly over us pore folks! He ain't such-a-much, nohow."

Minnie Westbrook, one of the younger girls who secretly had succumbed to the charms of the schoolmaster, came home that afternoon and reported to big, gloating Simon:

"You're not going to be any Santa Claus this time, Sim!" she said, with a certain ferocity.

"Who said I won't!" bellowed Simon.

"*I* said you won't!"

"Yah, I guess you're boss man of the works, eh? Well, I'll pull your pigtails out and throw you in the creek, if you get sassy with Sim Westbrook. I'll reach down and gnaw off two-three acres of that bigoted upper lip of your'n. How come I won't be Santa? I already asked Squire Jesse Leverage, and he never said no word against it."

"Well, Judge Jesse he's gone away till after Christmas, and gave 'Fessor Dave the right to name his own Santa!"

"What?" barked Simon.

"I told you!" said the girl fiercely. "You just made a mess of things, and yourself, too, when you started that lawsuit!"

His dark face went a curious gray, then became swept with the swarth of chagrined anger. "Say—" began Simon; then he fell to raving and growling. "So that's the way he worked to get it back on me! He knowed I wanted to be that Santy. He knowed good and well it's my job. I been so now for eight years. Everybody in the settlement knows it's my job. The suit fits me like it was made for me. I do it far better than any other person in these parts. Dave Conley knows that. He knows how I feel. Now—great guns!" He stopped, glaring at his sister, as if she might have some part in it. "I'm half a mind to box your jaws! I'm going to see the other members of the school board."

"Well, I hope they don't give it to you!"

"You say that again, and I'll snatch you bald-headed."

"I hope," said the girl, "they don't give it to you! You're just plain mean and small, that's what, Sim Westbrook! If you had an inch of real man in you, you'd go straight to Grandpap Westbrook and have that case thrown out of court, and you'd go to that Christmas tree and apologize in public for what you've done!"

"I'm a mind to wring your neck!" He did nothing of the kind; instead, he hurried out, saddled his mule, and rode furiously away to interview the other members of the school board.

He came back, after an hour, looking glum and browbeaten. He had talked with Mr. Walker and Luke Sardis, the other members; they said it was Judge Jesse Leverage's job to look after that. If Judge Jesse had empowered Mr. Dave to get his Santa, then Mr. Dave should get him, and that was all there was of it.

To anyone not familiar with the single-track mountaineer mind it would be difficult to understand how desperately upset Simon Westbrook was by the turn of events. Few honors were to be had in the simplicity of life in Poverty Run and Chittling Meat Mountain. The adults divided the honors of magistrate's office, constable and school board among them. Little was left for an arrogant, power-hungry young fellow like Simon Westbrook. Moreover, he was the best Santa that could be had in that locality. The honest truth was, he was a genuine artist at it!

Now he had played havoc. He had lost the single great honor that he wanted, above all others available to him. He could not humble himself to Dave Conley, however. That would have been unthinkable. He beat his hands together, and moaned, walking up and down the big puncheon-floored room of the mountain dwelling.

"I wisht I'd never have started this mess! I wisht that idiot of Dave Conley had a-left that tree alone, then I wouldn't done this! I'm of a mind to go hunt him up and beat his head for him. It was all his fault!"

"It's your fault!" accused his sister.

"Look here! You going back on your own blood and kin on account of that there feller?"

"I aim to be fair. All the pupils are crazy about 'Fessor Dave. He's nice, and he's smart, and he's good. He wouldn't ever have sworn out a warrant for you, Sim! If he'd been back of that tree, watching you cut a tree on his land, he'd have yelled out to you, 'Don't do that, Sim!' or, more apt, he'd have come on down and said, 'Take it. It's a nice tree. I'm glad I can give it to you and to the school. Here, let me help you cut it and load it.' That's what he'd have said, I think!"

Simon glowered at Minnie, in baffled rage. "You done fell in love with the teacher! Think of that!"

"No!" she denied swiftly. "But I've got a right to like somebody that I ought to like."

"I'm going to hunt that feller up and have this thing out with him!" The matter had resolved itself in Simon's mind as a personal issue. He went to the door and took the gun from the horns above. Minnie undertook to wrestle the weapon from him, but he flung her backward, and strode out into the falling dusk. A light snow was falling; the wind was bitter in its knife thrusts. Simon Westbrook, but dimly aware he was making an idiot of himself, walked quickly down the school path.

He thought that he probably would find young Dave there, working on the tree. Christmas Eve would be tomorrow night. Tomorrow night! He stumbled. The wind held him back; then he took a fresh grip on his anger, and pushed on.

Men had killed each other for less. The Mosley-Westbrook feud, famous in its day, had cost a score of lives over the years on a pretext no more valid than Simon Westbrook's. The excuse does not count much in anger; the condition of mind and drive of anger is all that counts. This set and drive carried Simon Westbrook on.

He saw a dim, muscular form take shape in the twilight of ghostly snow. Simon Westbrook stopped. The figure came up the trail, carrying some sort of parcel. Simon stiffened all through his great frame, and he brought the gun to rest in the bend of his arm.

"Howdy," he snarled, standing in the middle of the path.

"Well, how're you?"

Although Dave Conley was startled by this unexpected encounter with Simon Westbrook his voice was still quiet and pleasant. He saw that Simon was armed. In that grim, swift moment, the schoolmaster sensed that Simon was after him.

Young Westbrook stood erect. "I—I—" he said, through set teeth; "I could kill you!" The barrel of the gun came gently to a point where it covered Dave Conley.

"Why, certainly," agreed Dave, and he was glad that his voice was natural and pleasant, though he knew a quarrel was inevitable, and that it would almost as inevitably cause this simple fellow to kill him. "I suppose," he went on quietly, "you could take that gun, and kill the next dozen men, women and children you met. What of it? It wouldn't show you up as much of a man."

"That's what you say!" snarled Simon.

"Anyway, what are you sore about? You had a right to prosecute me for getting that tree. I had no legal right to go on your land and take what was yours. I'm not kicking. I could have wished that the whole unfortunate matter was otherwise, but I cannot deny those rights that are so patently yours. And about acting Santa Claus, I've brought the suit to you."

Simon looked dazed, and he eyed the bundle with befuddled eyes. "That?"

"That's it. You're the best man for the job. You're an artist at it in fact, Simon. You're not much on the peace-on-earth-good-will-toward-men side of it, going around here toting guns to shoot unarmed schoolteachers. But I have to admit the truth and say that you're the finest Santa I ever saw or heard of. So, I kept thinking, and I finally made up my mind that I could do nothing except give the job to the one best suited for it, whether I liked you or not, personally, Simon. The truth is, I don't. I can't, but I believe that I can be honest with myself and you, and at the same time give you the job I know you want.

"Here's the suit." Dave put it in Simon's limp arms. "I suppose some folks will say that I'm acting the coward, trying to buy off your anger. It may be, Simon, you will think so. I can't help what others say. I hope that I am anything but a coward. I'm asking you to take your old place for no reason in the world save that you're by far the best for it. The job is small; I think the principle of the thing is very great." He turned after a moment, leaving the dazed Simon standing in the snowy gloom, and retraced his steps.

The next evening the crowd came early to the schoolhouse, and soon the room was packed. The tree was genuinely beautiful in its decorations and burden of presents. Santa was late. When he entered, he was badly out of breath. In his vigorous, robust voice, curiously changed from the tense savage tone Dave had last heard, Santa said, "I been late, I had to stop down beyond the fence row and pray a spell. Pray for this here Christmas season, pray for all you leetle chaps and the big folks too; but mostly I had to get on my hunkers and pray for myself. And I had a right smart rassle with the bad in myself, at that. I don't mind telling all you folks—big ones and little ones, too. Some will know better than others what I mean. But this here thing we call Christmas is time for peace and good will. And I ain't been so peaceful, in my heart, and they ain't been such a power of good will in me—till I had it out just now in the fence corner. So, before Santa starts giving out the presents, I got a few different kinds of presents to give.

"Take this here lovely tree, chilluns. It belonged, so I hear tell, to a low-down, mean-headed feller named Simon Westbrook. He got a lawsuit going over it, against the schoolteacher. Well, Santa went to the jedge and say to the jedge, 'Throw that case out of co't.' So the jedge he say, 'Okeh, I'll throw it out of co't.' And he did. Now, me, Santa, gives the tree to the school and the 'fessor. And the 'fessor, I might as well tell you all, is a right smart feller. He teeched a grand school here, and will keep on at such. Now, let's give all of you a pretty gift!"

What it cost Simon Westbrook to say this not many would ever know. Dave Conley knew; he was sensitive to human ways, and he appreciated with keen depth the greatness that Simon showed. Perhaps no one else than Dave could have caused this change, for that was a part of the young schoolmaster's genius. At any rate the yuletide spirit prevailed—peace on earth, and good will toward men.

The wintry wind, whipping the eaves of the old schoolhouse, seemed to repeat it:

Peace on earth . . . good will toward men. . . .

Harry Harrison Kroll

Indiana-born Harry Harrison Kroll, besides being a linguist, was the author of several books, including *The Cabin in the Cotton, Lost Homecoming,* and *Riders in the Night.* He also wrote many short stories.

CHRISTMAS BELLS

Seth Parker

NO MAN NEED
WALK ALONE

For ten years now, readers have kept our mailbox full by continuing to send us stories. This old story is one that just keeps coming. Evidently there's something about Old Hitch that tugs at the heart. Without question, this is the write-in story of the year!

J don't suppose you ever knew Esau Tinker, but he was a tall gawky feller and owned the General Store down at the Corners. He was a real nice gentleman, as gentlemen go, but apt to be a little noisy and quite a galavanter. Didn't have any use for religion. The Parson would try and talk with Esau and so would the Deacons, but it wasn't any use. Nobody could ever seem to quite get inside his skin.

Well, one year just before Christmas, Esau was up in the garret looking for some of the last year's red and green paper and tinsels, and he came across an old newspaper, 'most twenty years old. He picked it up and read it over and it tickled his funny bone so that he brought it down to the store and put it on the counter among the Christmas supplies where folks would see it. They'd come to do their shopping and look over the toys and the choc'late Santa Clauses and the like of that, and then they'd spy the paper; thinking it was the last edition they'd pick it up and sometimes scan it over quite a spell before they'd catch on to its being an old one. Esau, he'd just sit back and watch them, and when they caught on, wouldn't he laugh!

Now, Esau kept the paper there for quite a few days and most of the folks in town had been in buying presents and had been fooled and so the novelty was kind of wearing off, when Esau chanced to look out the window and he saw Old Hitch Thomas coming along on his old peg leg. The old gentleman lived about two miles out of town in a little shack way back in the woods and he didn't come in to do any buying except about every five or six months, but I imagine he knew about its being Christmas and that everybody was doing some shopping and selling. As he didn't have anybody to give presents to he reckoned that he might as well come in and buy himself some beans and flour and at least have the fun of doing something for the holidays. He was just one of these poor unfortunates who ain't necessary to nobody else and so the folks in town had just come to look on him as an outsider. And Christmastime to an outsider can be the lonesomest time of the year.

Well, when Esau saw him headed for the store he tipped the boys off not to say a word about the paper, and while Old Hitch was stocking up on vittles he chanced to look at the paper. Picked it up and read it real serious and seemed to puzzle a mite, and then he laid it down again, and when his vittles was wrapped up he paid for them and went out without saying a word. The boys laughed fit to kill because Old Hitch hadn't even caught on that it was an old paper.

Well, a couple of days later, the day before Christmas to be exact, when Esau was opening up the store about six in the morning, he looked down the road and there was Old Hitch swinging along on his wooden leg, and tucked under his arm was a crutch. Hitch has had a leg of timber ever since anybody in these parts knew him and Esau wondered what he was carrying a crutch under his arm for unless it was to use like a spare tire if the leg gave out on him; but he didn't think any more about it and went on tending the store.

That night, though, along about nine, as he was closing up, he looked down the road again and there, plugging along through the snow and making pretty poor head-way, was Old Hitch Thomas. He was whistling, happy as a lark, but Esau thought he was walking kind of funny,

and when he got nearer he could see why. Hitch only
had one leg and he was swinging himself along as best he
could with the crutch under the off arm.

"Hello, Hitch," says Esau. "What's ailing you?"

"Nothing," says Old Hitch, swinging up on his crutch.
"Feeling chip as a cricket. Never felt better in my life."

"But where's your wooden leg?" says Esau, "Lost it
in the snow?"

"No," says Hitch, "I didn't lose it. But you know
that paper you had on the counter the other day?"

Esau allowed that he remembered, so Hitch continued. "When I was buying the vittles in your place, I
took a look at it and I seen something I couldn't get
over. No sir, I tried my best but I couldn't."

"What did you see?" says Esau, not quite so comfortable now.

"I saw that notice in there," says Old Hitch, "about
that little boy who was run over by the jigger wagon
and had his leg jammed so bad that they had to cut it
off. Then it went on to say how poor the family was
and it would be nice if someone could see the little
feller got a wooden leg so he could run about and do
things. Said he lived almost twelve miles out on the
river road in the house that sets back on the bank."

Esau made a queer noise with his throat you could
have took for anything from "yes" to coughing.

"Well," says Old Hitch, "when I got back home I
commenced thinking about that little feller. Seeing I
was a boy myself when I lost my leg I knew how he
must be feeling, and as I'm pretty old and have the
rheumatis anyhow and can't get around much, I picked
up this morning, and walked out to where the paper

said he lived. There weren't anybody to home and the place looked pretty deserted, but I calc'lated they must be away for the day somewhere. Anyhow I took my leg off and had some green and red ribbon with me and tied it to the front door. I reckon he'll be pretty tickled when he comes home, don't you think so?"

Esau just stood there, and he couldn't have said a word if his life depended upon it; he knew the little feller had died years before, and the family had moved away a long time ago, but he would have cut his tongue out before he would have told Old Hitch, who had walked that day close to twenty-eight miles to give his wooden leg to a little boy on Christmas.

"Well," says Hitch, swinging himself upon his crutch again, "I guess I'll be getting on."

But before he left he put his hand on Esau's shoulder and said, "Esau, I was all alone when I walked over and left my peg leg for him, but on the way back I ain't been walking alone. No sir, I ain't been walking alone." And with a wave of his hand and a smile on his face, Old Hitch swung off for his little cabin home back in the woods.

And as Esau stood there, the tears rolled down his cheeks as he watched the old man swing himself along as best he could on one leg and a wooden crutch. And as he stood there that Christmas Eve the bells in the church started to ring out the glad tidings, and Esau dropped to his knees to make a Christmas present of his heart to the One who had walked back with Old Hitch Thomas.

Seth Parker
Nothing is known of Seth Parker today.

Frank V. McMillan

TERRY

---

*In Miss Dickson's second grade class were thirty
children, each with needs that must be met. Since so
many underprivileged children filled these seats, all
the teachers had been warned—warned to keep their
emotional distance. With the other children this was
difficult enough; but with Terry—well, that's the
story.*

❄ ❄ ❄

*This fairly recent story, I predict, will go on to become
one of our most-loved Christmas stories.*

*J*f Terry had any look about him at all, it would be called *hungry*. That was Miss Dickson's view of him. In her class of thirty children, each was no stranger to want and hard times, but Terry's need was most obvious. He'd been turned back to the Good Shepherd Home by his third set of foster parents.

There were times during the teaching day, quiet, reflective times, with all the small heads bent in fierce concentration over workbooks, when something would make her look up from the papers she was grading and her eyes would meet Terry's. His curly blond head would drop back almost immediately to his notebook, but she would be shaken by the longing plea in those large gray eyes, by the hunger that lingered in them. Not for food, although these children were poor. It wasn't Terry's stomach that was empty.

It was Miss Dickson's first class, these second graders. She'd been warned, as had the other teachers newly assigned to this underprivileged neighborhood school, not to let the kids get to them. They'd be quick to pick up on any display of sympathy.

"They'll take advantage of you," the principal, Mr. Bevans, warned. "Don't let them get too close."

One hot, stifling morning the school secretary handed her each child's folder. By the end of the day the reading material had left her far more emotionally drained than she was physically from the hot, cramped office.

Most of the children were from broken homes or were staying with foster parents. They lived in low-income, shabby apartments.

Terry's intelligence was exceptionally high, but he

was classed as a student who was not doing the work he was capable of doing.

On the first day of school Miss Dickson asked each child to print his or her first name and last initial on a strip of paper she had placed on the desk, and then to pin the strips on their shirts or dresses so that she could learn their names quickly. Even before Terry so identified himself, she knew who he was. He was the first one in the room that morning, and he chose the desk closest to hers.

His hair was still damp, and had been combed so painstakingly that each strand seemed to have a separate life of its own.

She noticed that very first morning the expression in his eyes that seemed to say, *Are you the one who will give me what I need?* She noticed it and understood it, and then quickly looked away.

When she assigned their permanent desks, she kept Terry up near the front of the room. She justified this by telling herself he was so small he might not be able to see well if he was sitting in the rear.

There were very few children in the class who approached him intellectually. It didn't take Miss Dickson long to discover he was able to read on a fourth-grade level. However, his arithmetic skills were poor, and his oral work in the classroom was far below what could reasonably be expected of him.

One noontime about halfway into the term, she was doing some paperwork at the desk while the children, finished with lunch, drifted out to the playground. At one point she lifted her head to find them all gone. All except Terry. He'd finished eating, the empty brown paper bag folded neatly on top of his desk, and was sitting there very quietly, looking at her.

"Aren't you going out to play, Terry?"

"No, Miss Dickson."

She glanced out the window that overlooked the small paved area where several pieces of play equipment were set up.

"It's a beautiful day, Terry. It would do you good to run and play with the other children." She smiled. "Make you feel more wide awake for the rest of the afternoon."

He blushed, and those amazing eyes of his slid away from her look for a moment and then returned.

"I'd rather stay here with you, Miss Dickson." He swallowed with a deep noisy gulp and looked down at his hands folded primly on the desk. "Could I erase the blackboards for you?"

There was something terribly vulnerable about the top of that small blond head with the ears sticking out on either side like teacup handles. The words *Mother dead, whereabouts of father unknown* flashed into her mind in large red letters, and she longed to go to Terry, put her arms around him, and tell him they would erase the boards together. Instead, she remembered Mr. Bevans' words about not letting the kids get close to you. She made her voice very cool and told him he couldn't reach high enough and to go out and get some fresh air.

He obeyed without saying anything further, and when she looked out the window, he had joined in a game of ball in one corner of the playground. She watched him for a few minutes, and although there was

nothing unusual about his behavior with the other children, she felt uneasy and not at all pleased with herself.

The weeks swept by, filled with both the frustrations
and satisfactions of teaching. But the war within her
went on as well: between Terry's need, which seemed
to be more acute each day, and about which she wanted
to do something, and the echoes of words heard many
times from more experienced teachers about not
becoming emotionally involved with pupils—especially
these pupils; about how they will take advantage if you
do. The echoes were loud, and they were winning.

For financial reasons the school policy was to observe
Christmas with a minimum of festivity and to discour-
age the exchanging of gifts. With this in mind, Miss
Dickson announced to the class that on the last day of
school before the holidays they would sing carols, and
each child could place a Christmas card under the small
tree she had brought.

After the children had finished their lunches on that
long-awaited day, she took the little tree out of her
closet, and a chorus of *oh*s filled the room. The tree was
short but bushy, trimmed with decorations of all colors,
topped with a silver angel with sparkling wings. A string
of flickering lights blinked shyly between the branches.

Miss Dickson reached under her desk and pulled out
a box filled with red stockings, fat and bulging with
candy and cookies.

She smiled down at their radiant faces. "All right,
children, come up front, place your card under the tree,
and take one of the stockings."

There was a ripple of pleasure, and the first row did

just that, the girls touching the tree ornaments lovingly as they passed.

Terry's row was next, and the little girl who sat in back of him prodded him with her fingers. But he just sat there in that characteristic pose of his, face bent over folded hands. When she saw he wasn't going to get up, Miss Dickson told Janie to lead her row up to the tree, and in a little while all the children except Terry had left their cards and received their Christmas stocking. After singing the familiar carols, she told the class they could leave early and wished them all a merry Christmas, feeling a deep pang as she contrasted their holiday with the preparations that were waiting for her younger brother and sister.

Terry got up too and went to get his coat, and although she pretended to be busy clearing off her desk, she watched as he lingered near the closet, buttoning and unbuttoning his coat and shifting his cap around on his head as though trying to find the most comfortable position. Finally, when the last "Merry Christmas, Miss Dickson" had been said by the last child, Terry approached the desk, and she held his stocking out to him.

"This is for you, Terry, and I do hope you have a very merry Christmas."

His hand reached out for the stocking, and she noticed it was shaking. She wondered how her throat could possibly have stretched to the point where it could accommodate the large rock she seemed to have acquired there. She wanted to tell this small, forlorn little boy that it didn't matter at all that he hadn't brought a card. There were so many things she wanted to say to Terry, but she was afraid to trust her voice, so she just watched as he put the stocking with the Christmas goodies on his desk, and then reached inside his jacket pocket to remove a small package tied with a red string.

"This is for you, Miss Dickson." The words were barely audible.

"Terry, remember how we agreed on cards for the holiday?"

"Yes, Miss Dickson." His voice was a whisper now.

She swallowed, but the boulder refused to move. "Terry, if you don't have a card for me, it's perfectly all right."

"I wanted to give you a present. Not just a card. A real present."

"Do you think it's fair to you to give me a present when the other children—"

He broke in as though the words had been held back by a dam that suddenly crumbled.

"It was my mother's. The lady at the Home told me she used to like it very much." And then slowly, "I wanted you to have it because I think you will like it very much."

Now it was Miss Dickson's turn to have trembling hands as she untied the string and lifted the lid of the little white box. Inside, on a piece of rough cotton, lay a small, heart-shaped locket, decorated with petals and leaves in pastel colors. There was a loop of metal on the top for a chain. She looked at him helplessly, not knowing what to say.

Terry grinned. "It opens! Press that little thing on the side, Miss Dickson."

She did and it snapped open.

"See?" he said, pointing a trembling finger. "You can put two pictures in it. One on each side. There was a picture of my father on one side, but I took it out. So now you can put your own picture in. And your father's and mother's." He took a deep breath. "Do you like it all right?"

"Oh, Terry." She touched his head briefly and then took her hand away. "It's beautiful. And I do like it very much. Just as your mother did. But, dear, I can't keep it. I'm sure someone in your family would be upset if you gave it away. I'm not a part of your family. It just wouldn't be right for me to take it."

"But, Miss Dickson . . ." He was so full of what he wanted to say, but he couldn't seem to get anything out but her name. She started to put the locket back in the box, but his voice stopped her.

"I don't have a family, Miss Dickson. There's just my father, and no one knows where he is. Anyway, he wouldn't care about the locket. He's forgot all about it, just like he forgot about me." He was saying these heart-breaking words without fully realizing what they meant.

"Miss Dickson, if you put your mother's picture and your father's picture in the locket, then it will be like a family. I didn't have a picture of my mother, so one side was empty. But you could fill it."

The brightness of his eyes had become liquid now. He was crying and snuffling in that special way little boys have, wiping his eyes and nose with the sleeve of his coat.

"Oh, dear God," she said half aloud. *Here I go. And I'm going to ask the Home if he can come to my house for Christmas. And I'm going out tonight and buy him some toys and clothing, something for everyone in the family to give him. And books. Not just picture books, but ones with words in them that he'll have to ask the meaning of, books that will challenge his quick, wonderful mind. And by the time he falls asleep on Christmas Eve he's going to know he's loved.*

Her training told her not to get involved in this little fellow's life. But then she thought, *What are emotions for if not to involve us with life and people? To help us know and recognize need in others, and to give of ourselves?*

She had to smile at such large thoughts applied to such a very small boy. She turned that smile to Terry.

He saw the smile and rushed into her arms, "Miss Dickson?"

"Yes, Terry."

"Miss Dickson. Would you be my mama?"

Tears were rolling down her face, but she didn't care.

"Terry," she said. "Thank you for the wonderful locket. I have a small picture of both my mother and father together that I can put on one side. Now I want a picture of you for the other side." She held the sobbing little boy tight in her arms. "Terry, you know what?"

"What, Miss Dickson?"

"Terry, honey, . . . I want very much to be your mama."

Frank V. McMillan

Frank V. McMillan was a freelance writer who wrote from Oregon until his recent death.

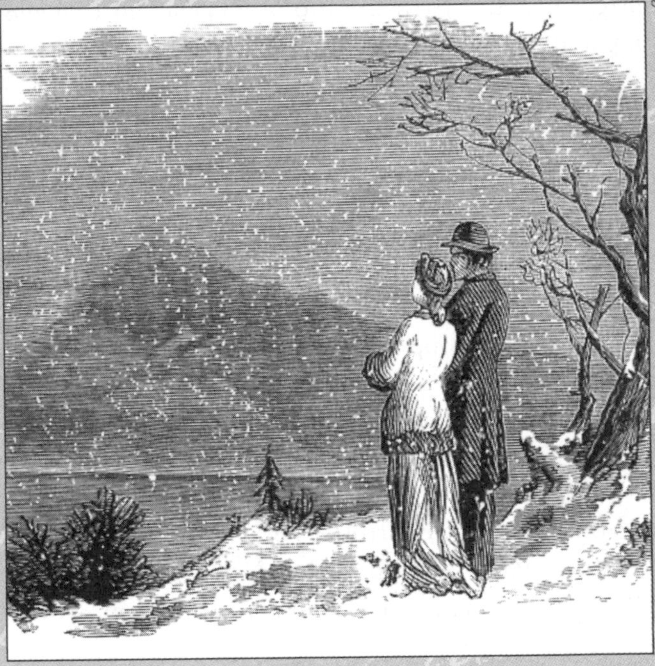

Pearl S. Buck

SECRETS OF THE HEART

---

*It was almost Christmas and her children and grand-
children wanted her, but she turned them down.
There was a journey she felt impelled to make.*
  Alone.

❋ ❋ ❋

*This is one of those rare Christmas stories penned for
those who have loved greatly and for those who wish
to remember. It is a love story like no other.*

*M*rs. Allenby listened to her daughter's plans for the holiday, and then it was time for her to make her announcement. "I won't be here for Christmas," Mrs. Allenby said, keeping her voice as casual as she could.

Her daughter Margaret stared at her. "What *do* you mean?" Margaret demanded. "It's impossible! Not here for Christmas? Where are you going?"

"I haven't decided," Mrs. Allenby said. She carefully tied a silver bow on a small package. Inside was a brooch for Margaret, a circle of pearls set in gold that she had found only yesterday in an antique shop. When the package was tied to her satisfaction she handed it to her daughter.

"For you—not to be opened until. . . . I'll deliver the other gifts for all of you, parents and children, to each of your houses before I go."

Margaret, about to leave after an hour of lively talk, sat down again in the blue velvet chair by the fire. They were in her mother's living room. The December sun was blazing through the windows, paling the flames that were crackling in the low grate.

"But, Mother, you've never been away at Christmastime!" Margaret cried.

"So this year I shall be," Mrs. Allenby said, her voice pleasant but firm.

She leaned back in her own blue velvet chair opposite and gazed at her daughter affectionately. "You're putting on a little weight, aren't you, dear?"

"Don't try to change the subject," Margaret said. "No, I'm not putting on weight and I'm *not* pregnant, if that's what you mean. Four children are enough—

though I'd rather enjoy a baby again! Benjie will be starting school next year and the house will be empty. But back to you now—when are you going?"

"I haven't decided," Mrs. Allenby said. "Perhaps tomorrow but perhaps not until Christmas Eve. I'll see when I get ready."

"I shan't enjoy Christmas, at all," Margaret said rather shortly.

"You will," Mrs. Allenby said. "And I suggest that you take the opportunity of my absence and not have the other families with you. Four of you, with your accumulated children, adorable as they are—well, it's simply too much, even of those adorable grandchildren."

"Mother, if I didn't know you love us—"

Mrs. Allenby interrupted. "Indeed, I love you all, but I think you should be alone for Christmas, each pair of parents with their own children, the children alone with only their own parents and brothers and sisters. You've no idea—" She stopped.

"Idea of what?" Margaret demanded, her eyes very blue under her dark hair. She was a small creature, but possessed of a mighty spirit. Hot or cold, she was all extremes.

"How peaceful it would be," Mrs. Allenby said rather lamely.

Her daughter looked at her critically. "You aren't being noble or something, are you? Thinking we don't want you or something stupid like that?"

"Oh no, indeed," Mrs. Allenby said. "Nothing like that."

Margaret was silent for a full half-minute, regarding

her mother with suspicious eyes. "You aren't carrying on some sort of secret romance?"

Mrs. Allenby blushed. "Margaret, how *can* you—"

"You *are!*" Margaret cried.

"I am *not,*" Mrs. Allenby said flatly. "At my age," she added.

"You're still pretty," Margaret said.

"Oh, nonsense," Mrs. Allenby said.

Margaret looked at her mother fondly and then rose. "Well, keep your secrets, but I still tell you I shan't enjoy Christmas for a minute, wondering where you are." She put her arms about her mother and kissed her. "And this present—the package is so small I know it's expensive and you shouldn't have. . . ."

"It's my money, darling," Mrs. Allenby said, laughing.

Margaret kissed her mother again, ran to the door and stopped to look back. "Tell me where you're going," she asked again, her voice coaxing.

Mrs. Allenby laughed. "Go home and tend your children," she said gaily and waved good-bye.

Alone with the fire, the winter sun streaming across the Aubusson carpet, the bowl of holly on the table, the book-lined walls, Mrs. Allenby was suddenly aware of a deep relief. She loved her house, she loved her children and their children, but—but what? She did not know what came after this *but.* Simply that she longed not to be here on Christmas. She would leave early in the morning of Christmas Eve. That would see her at the cabin in Vermont by nightfall. Now she rose, gathered some bits of silver cord and wrapping paper, which she threw into the fire, and went upstairs to pack.

By eight the morning of Christmas Eve she was in

her car and headed north. Snow threatened from a
smooth gray sky, and in Vermont, the radio told her,
it was already snowing. They had often gone skiing in
Vermont in the old days, she and Leonard, before they
were married. And it was to Vermont that they had
gone for their honeymoon, but in October, and too
early for skiing. How glorious it had been, nevertheless,
the mountains glittering in scarlet and gold!

"In celebration of our wedding," Leonard had said.

It was because of him, of course, that she wanted to
have Christmas alone, and in Vermont. They had always
come here alone. It had been his demand.

"Let's never go to Vermont with the children—
always alone," he had said.

"Selfish, aren't you," she had teased, with love.

"Plenty of other places to ski with them," he had
retorted.

"Of course we mustn't let them know—they'd be
hurt," she had said.

"No reason why they should know this place even
exists," he had agreed.

That was just after they had built the cabin and now it
was the place essential to her, for there she could refresh,
revitalize, her memory of Leonard. She was frightened
because she was forgetting him, losing him—not the sum
total of him, of course, but the clarity of detail of his
looks, the dark eyes and the sandy hair. He had died so
heartbreakingly young, the children still small, and their
own children never to see their grandfather—see the way
he walked, his tall spare frame moving in his own half-
awkward, curiously graceful fashion. The memory came
strong at Christmas, especially—he had loved sprawling

on the floor with his children, showing them how to play with the toys he chose for them with such care.

The snow was beginning to fall now, a few flakes, growing heavier as she drove out of the traffic and toward the mountains. She would reach the cabin late this evening. Leonard had designed the cabin before any of the children were born so it had only three rooms. He had not wanted children too soon.

"Let's be solid with each other first," he had said.

They had come to the cabin often during the first years of their life together, as often as he could get away from the laboratories where he worked as a research scientist. After the children came, it was less often and at last, when he was dead, not at all—that is, she had never come back alone. Yet she had not thought of selling it. Gradually she had not thought of it at all, though she knew now she had not forgotten it.

The hours sped past. She was a fast driver but steady, Leonard always said, and it was she who usually did the driving when they went to the cabin, the quiet hours giving him time to think. He had said gratefully, "What it means to a man like me not to have to talk—"

Yet, some laboratory problem solved, he would be suddenly gay with lively talk. They had good talk together, and it was not until his voice was stilled in death that she realized how good the talk was, and that there always had been something to talk about.

The day slipped past noon, and the snow continued to fall. Before darkness fell she reached the village and there she stopped to buy food for a day or two. The old storekeeper was gone, and a young man, a stranger, had taken his place. He looked at her curiously but asked no

questions as he carried the box of groceries to her car.
She drove on then in the dusk, up the winding graveled
road to the tip of the snow-covered hill. The road
narrowed, and within a few yards she saw the cabin.
The trees had grown enormous, but the cabin was still
there, as enduring as Leonard had planned it to be.

She got out of the car and lifted a flat stone. Yes, the
key was still there, too, the big brass key.

"I hate little keys," Leonard had said. "They lose
themselves on purpose."

So they had found the huge, old brass lock, a heavy
and substantial one. She fitted the key into the hole, and
the door creaked open. *Dear God, it couldn't be the same
after all these years*—but it *was* the same.

"We must always leave it as though we were coming
back tomorrow," Leonard had said.

It was dusty, of course, and it smelled of the forest and
dead leaves. But it had been built so solidly that bird and
beast had found no entrance. The logs in the great fireplace were ready to light, and in the bedroom the bed
was made—damp and musty, doubtless, but there it was,
and the fire would soon drive out the dampness. She
would hang the bedclothes before the chimney piece.

She lit the fire and the big oil lamp, then she
unpacked the car, and sat down in the old rocking chair
to rest a few minutes before preparing food. So here she
was, unexpectedly really, for she had made no long-
standing plans to come here. It had come over her
suddenly, the need to find Leonard somehow, even to
remember him. And this had happened when she was
buying the brooch for Margaret. It had taken a little
time to find it.

"Are you looking for something for yourself?" the young woman in the antique shop had asked.

"No," she had replied, "I'm just looking."

"A tie pin for your husband, perhaps?" the young woman had persisted.

"I have no husband," she had replied, shortly. Then she had corrected herself. "I mean—he died many years ago."

But her instinctive reply had frightened her. No husband—was she forgetting Leonard? Impossible—but perhaps true? And here it was Christmas again, and if ever he was not to be forgotten it was at Christmas, the time he loved best. And suddenly all her heart had cried out for him. Yet where was he to be found, if not in memory? And suddenly she needed to be alone this Christmas. The children, grown into men and women, and their children, whom he had never seen, were strangers to him; and living in their midst, she had almost allowed herself to become a stranger to him, too.

She got up to open a can of soup and put it on the stove. Then she found the dust cloths in a drawer where she had folded them, freshly washed, and she dusted the furniture before she ate. The fire was roaring up the chimney and the room had lost its chill. The snow was falling more heavily now and by morning it would be piled against the door. The main road would be plowed, however, since there were many new houses for skiers who had started coming here in increasing numbers— she had read of that. And Leonard always saw to it that the snow shovel hung inside the shed at the end of the cabin.

She pulled the small drop-leaf table before the fire

and set out her supper, a bowl of bean soup, bread and cheese and fruit, and she ate with appetite. When she had eaten she folded the table away against the wall. Then she heated water and took her bath in a primitive tin tub. It was all so easy, so natural, to do what they had done, she and Leonard, here alone in the forest. Clean and warm in her flannel nightgown she went in to the bed, now warm and dry, but still smelling of autumn leaves, and fell into dreamless sleep.

She woke the next morning to sunshine glittering upon new-fallen snow. For a moment she didn't know where she was. Here, where she had always been with Leonard, her right hand reached for him instinctively. Then she remembered. It was Christmas Day and she was alone. No, not alone, for her first thought summoned Leonard to her mind. She lay for a moment in the warm bed. Then she spoke.

"I can talk out loud here—there is no one to hear me and wonder."

She heard her own voice and was comforted by its calm. "I can talk all I want to out loud," she went on.

A pleasant peace crept into her heart and body, as gentle as a perfume, and she smiled.

"We spent our first Christmas here," she reminded herself.

They had driven up through snow flurries that year, and, as she had done, only together, they had waked to another day of sun upon snow. Then Leonard had got up to light the fire and heat the water.

"Lie still, sweetheart," he had commanded. "There's no one here to hurry us—a glorious Christmas Day."

He had come back to bed, shivering, and they had begun the day with love.

Later they had breakfasted on the small table before the fire, and while she washed the dishes, he had gone out and cut a little tree and had brought it in, glistening with ice, and they had decorated it. They had remembered to bring tinsel and a few silver ornaments, and they had tied their gifts to the branches.

"I've planned every moment of this day," he had said. When they had admired the tree, they opened their presents. She had given him a gold band for his wristwatch and he had given her a necklace that was a delicate silver chain.

"To bind you to me forever," he had said, slipping it over her head.

She had loved the chain through all the years and wore it often. She had even brought it with her, to wear with her red wool dress today. Remembering, she got up from the bed and ran into the other room to build the fire.

She laid bits of bark and slivers of dry wood on the lingering coals. She had made such a mighty fire last night that under the ashes there were still live coals. In a few minutes the blaze sprang up in sharp flickering points. Leonard had taught her how to make a proper fire that first year, and she had never forgotten.

She filled the big kettle now with water from the kitchen pump and hung it on the crane above the fire. When the water was hot she washed and dressed, putting on her red dress, and sat down at the table for breakfast. And when she finished eating and washed the dishes, she put on Leonard's lumber jacket, which hung as usual behind the door, and went out to cut a tree—a very tiny one, just to set on the table. The tree ornaments were where Leonard had put them, years ago, in the wall drawer under the window, and she tied them on the tree. Then she found the gift she brought for herself in her bag, and she tied it to the tree.

"A year or two and perhaps there'll be more than the two of us," Leonard had said, on their third Christmas. "We've had over two years alone. Now let's have our children—four of them—close together while we're still young. They can enjoy each other and us, and there'll be years for us alone after they've grown up and don't need us any more."

"We can't bring a baby to this cabin in the middle of winter," she had said.

"We'll take Christmas where we find it," he had told her.

And sharing his desire, as she loved to do because she loved him, by the next Christmas they had a son, named for his father but called Lennie. He was three months old that Christmas and they spent it, the three of them, in their first house, a modest one on a quiet street in the small Connecticut town where she still lived.

"I'm sure he sees the tree," Leonard had insisted.

Lennie, lying on the rug, had stared steadily at the glittering tree, still not a very big tree but one loaded with gifts. Then he had smiled, and both she and Leonard had laughed and reached for each other's hand.

"I'm glad we're alone, the three of us," Leonard had said. "It's selfish of me not to want to go to either of our parents', but we have our own home now, you and I and our child. That's the trinity of love, my love."

In less than two years they had their daughter, Margaret.

"Another one and we'll need a bigger house," Leonard had said on Christmas Day.

Lennie, an accomplished walker by then, had been pulling things off the tree. Margaret had been propped on pillows on the couch.

"Oh Leonard, the payments on this one—" she had cried.

Before she could finish he had stopped her with a kiss: "A present for you, darling—I'm being promoted."

She had reproached him in her joy. "And you didn't tell me!"

"Christmas gift," he had said.

They had started to build their new house that next spring. By November it was still not quite finished but they moved in anyway to celebrate Dickie's birth.

"It was such an occasion," she said aloud now, smiling.

She noticed then that the fire was burning low, the logs mere coals and the ashes falling. She rose and got a new log from the stack, though it took all her strength to lift it.

"I wish you would realize you aren't a giant," Leonard had said so many times. "You're too impulsive— you see something you want done and you rush to do it yourself, forgetting that you have an able-bodied man around."

The log fell crookedly and she had to kneel to straighten it. Flames sprang from the coals and she dusted her hands and sat down again in the rocking chair.

That first Christmas in their new house had been a blessed one. Two little children ran about the room, shouting with delight, and Dickie sat propped on the couch. Lennie had his first tricycle and Margaret her first real doll. She loved dolls from that day on, and from them learned to love babies—nowadays her own. But little Dickie . . .

The tears were hot against her eyelids now and she bit her lip. There was more than joy to remember. There was also sorrow. Dickie had died before the next Christmas. Death had come suddenly, stealing into the house. She had put him to bed one night a few days before Christmas, and in the morning had gone to wake him and had found him dead. The beautiful body was there, white as the snow outside the window, and the blue eyes were still closed as if in sleep. Unpredicted, unexplained, and she still wept when she thought of it. She wept now as if she had lost him only yesterday. Back then she had known she must try to comfort Leonard, although in weeks upon weeks, he would not be comforted. But for his sake she had been compelled not to weep, compelled to seem brave when she was not brave.

"Don't even speak of Christmas," he had said that dreadful year. And against every beat of her own aching heart she had persuaded him.

"Dearest, there are the others. They've been looking forward to Christmas Day. We must go on as usual—as best we can."

"You are right, I know," he had said at last. "But don't expect too much of me."

They had both been glad when Christmas Day was over, that heartbreaking day.

"Oh, how did we ever . . ." she whispered now and sobbed.

It was still unendurable and she got up from the rocking chair.

"I shall make myself a cup of tea," she said aloud.

While the tea was steeping, she made herself a turkey sandwich from the sliced meat she had bought the day before. The sun was already past zenith and the room had lost its glow. When she had eaten the sandwich and had drunk her tea she felt better. She put another log on the fire and then she went to the window seat and sat looking out on the wintry landscape, the field covered with snow, the spruce forest tipped with snow, the white birch trees, and the peak of the mountain beyond, all drenched in the pure light of afternoon.

She and Leonard had endured that terrible Christmas, and in the spring she was pregnant again.

By the next Christmas Day, Ronald was born, and two years later Ellen.

"Enough," Leonard had told her, laughing. "You produce wonderful babies, my pet, but enough is enough."

So there had been no more and thereafter her Christmas Days became a blur of happiness, the kinds of celebration varying only with the ages of the children, gifts changing from toys to adolescent treasures and at last to young-adult possessions.

"I wish, Leonard darling, that you could have seen the first grandchild," she said now, her gaze fixed on the peak of the mountain, glowing in early sunset.

That would have been their happiest Christmas, the year Margaret's first child, Jimmy, was born, a little bundle of joy and mischief. Impossible to believe that now he was in college!

"You would have laughed all day, my darling, at his antics," she said aloud and laughed to herself at the very thought of what had never been.

❋ ❋ ❋

When the children were almost grown came the years when Leonard took her with him on business trips. He was the head of his own company by then and they had traveled to Europe and sometimes even to Asia. It had seemed to her that everyone treated her as though she were a queen, and that was because he was the king. But they had always managed to be home for Christmas, what with the children growing up and getting married, and she had talked of the grandchildren coming along, though Leonard had laughed at the idea of her being a grandmother.

"Didn't I tell you it was right for us to have the children when we were young? Now we can enjoy ourselves, doing whatever we like, for years to come."

Not so many years, at that, for nineteen years and thirteen days ago Leonard had come home at midday saying that he felt ill. His heart, so robust an organ all his life, had developed its own secret weakness, had suddenly stopped, beyond recall.

❋ ❋ ❋

She stared out the window now, as the shadows of evening crept over the landscape. There was nothing more to say, for long ago all questions had been asked and answered, in some fashion or other. Only the eternal *why* remained and to that there was no answer. She sat in silence but strangely comforted. She had wanted to remember him clearly, and in remembering, he had come back to her.

At this moment she heard a knock on the door. With no sense of alarm she opened it and saw a man standing there, a man with a graying beard.

"I'm Andrew Bond, ma'am, a neighbor. My wife says she saw smoke here and I thought I'd better come over."

She put out her hand. "Why, Andrew Bond, your father used to look after the cabin for us. You've forgotten."

He stared at her. "No, I haven't forgotten—but are you here alone, ma'am?"

"Yes, for the day, that is. I came just to—well, I just came."

"Yes, ma'am. So you aren't staying?"

"No, if you'll dig me out tomorrow morning?"

"Yes, ma'am, I'll be glad to."

"Will you come in?"

"No, thanks. Wife's got supper on and she doesn't like to wait!"

"Well, thank you for coming, Andrew. And I hope you had a merry Christmas."

"Well, my wife and me, we've had a happy Christmas, anyway. Our son come home from Vietnam—wounded, but alive."

"I'm glad he's alive," she said fervently, as though he were someone she knew. But she was really glad.

"Thank you, ma'am," he said. "I'll see you in the morning, ma'am."

"I'll see you in the morning," she echoed.

She closed the door and lit the lamp and heaved another log on the fire. She decided she would eat something and then go to bed early. Tomorrow she would be home again, ready to see them all, the children and their children. She had had her day, her Christmas Day. She went to the window and stood looking out into the gathering darkness. . . . Happy? Who knows what that is?

No, wounded—but alive!

Pearl S. Buck

Pearl S. Buck (1892–1973) towers over twentieth-century American writers, being one of the rare few to be awarded both the Pulitzer Prize and the Nobel Prize for Literature. Born in Hillsboro, West Virginia, she spent much of her early life in China. Her best-sellers include *The Good Earth*, *Dragon Seed*, *Peony*, and *Imperial Woman*.

Adeline Sergeant

WHILE SHEPHERDS
WATCHED

Tony's favorite thing in the world was music—a good thing, since his father was very poor in worldly possessions. Now it was Christmas once again, and by chance Tony's father was performing in the city where he grew up.

This gave Tony an idea.

❄ ❄ ❄

The setting is northern England in the 1890s.

A tall, spare, dark-eyed young man, with a violin case in his hand, came up the narrow stairs three steps at once, as though he were anxious to reach the little attic room which was his destination. There was a lamp in the hall below, but no light on the stairs or landings save the dim gleam which came through a skylight in the roof; and at six o'clock in the evening of the twenty-fourth of December, it is needless to remark that the top story was enveloped in total darkness. But Guy Fairfax seemed to know his way by instinct, and did not pause until he reached the scratched and shabby-looking door which formed the entrance to his abode. There he stopped short, waited, and listened for a moment, arrested by a sound that issued from the room.

It was the sound of a violin, faintly played, as though the instrument itself were small and the hand of the player weak. Presently there arose also a sweet little thread of a childish voice, singing to the tune picked out on the violin, the words of a well-known Christmas hymn:

> *"While shepherds watched their flocks by night,*
> *All seated on the ground."*

Guy's face contracted a little as if with pain; then he smoothed it resolutely, called up a smile, and opened the attic door.

It was a miserably bare room, not very clean nor very tidy, and the small fire that burned in the rusty grate did not avail to warm the atmosphere. On the bed, with an old fur cloak tucked round him for warmth, a little boy was curled up, his hands holding the tiny fiddle to the notes of which Guy had been listening. But he put it down at once and held out his hands with a crow of delight when Guy came in.

"Daddy! Daddy! Are you back so quick? I thought you wasn't coming till ever so long."

It was a sweet little voice, a sweet little face; but the lad's body was very frail and weak, and the dark eyes looked pathetically large for the delicate little face. It was with a sort of passionate yearning that Guy Fairfax pressed his child to his breast for a moment and then looked at him with a mournful foreboding which rendered his voice less cheerful than he meant it to be.

"I've run home for half an hour, Tony, to see that my boy is warm and comfortable," said the young man, folding the child close to him as he spoke.

"Oh, yes, I'm quite comfy," said Tony, contentedly. "I put on your old cloak and p'tended I was a bear; then I was a little choirboy singing carols in the street— Christmas carols, you know, Daddy, because Christmas is tomorrow, and it was tonight that the shepherds was watching their flocks—all seated on the ground—"

His voice passed almost unconsciously from speech to song. Indeed, although Tony was only six years old, singing was as natural to him as speech. He came of a musical race: his father was a musician, first by choice, then by necessity, and his mother, who died when he was only two years old, had been a professional singer, belonging to a family who had lived half their lives upon the operatic stage. Tony inherited her tastes, just as he inherited her golden hair, but he had his father's brow and his father's eyes.

"You like carols, Tony!"

"At Christmastime, Daddy. Will the singers come down this street tonight, do you think?"

"Perhaps so. There used to be plenty of them when I was a boy."

"You lived here, when you were a little boy like me, didn't you, Daddy?"

"Not here in the town, Tony. A little way outside— at the big house I've told you about before."

Tony regarded his father with baby seriousness. "Won't you take me to see it while we're here? Or is the company going away tomorrow?"

Fairfax belonged to a traveling operatic company, and could not afford to do otherwise than the other members of the troupe; but he would have given a good deal to find himself in any other place rather than the big, northern manufacturing town, where, unfortunately, his family had been well known for many generations. He had broken with his relations long ago—but—well, it was trying to find himself so near the dear old Grange where his father was still living, two miles outside the town, and not be able to go near him nor even let him know that his son and grandson were so near.

"I can't take you to see it," he said, in a low voice to the little son. "There—there wouldn't be time."

He was ashamed of the subterfuge as he looked into Tony's innocent eyes; but Tony was only half attending after all.

"And Santa Claus?" he said. "Will he come down the chiminey to give me things as he did you when you were a little boy?"

"Really, Tony, we must look after your English. Chiminey indeed! You know better than that."

"It don't matter," said Tony, fearlessly. "Will he come down it, that's what I want to know?"

"Not down attic-chimneys, I'm afraid," said the father, with a sigh.

"Oh–h!—But in at the door, maybe? Perhaps his sack would be too heavy for the chim-ney. He'll come all the way up the stairs, bump, bump, bumpity-bump, won't he?—and I shall stay awake and hear him."

"Better not," said Guy, rather sadly. "Santa Claus has forgotten us this year, mannie; he comes only to rich people."

"That's a shame," said Tony. "We aren't rich people, are we, Daddy?"

"Certainly not," answered the young man, thinking of the guinea a week which he was accustomed to receive on treasury day. "Not precisely rich, Tony; but not paupers—yet."

The bitter accent in his voice was caused by a vivid remembrance of some words that the angry old father had once addressed to him. "You need not darken my door again, sir; and when you and your wife are paupers, don't think that you'll get money out of me." The word *paupers* always recalled the bitterness of that moment to his mind.

"What's paupers?" said Tony. Then, in an abstracted tone, "I suppose Santa Claus always came to the big house where you lived."

"I suppose he did."

"And does he come still?"

"If there were any children there, I daresay he would."

"Oh," said Tony, with a very solemn face. Then he

said no more, but sat motionless, looking thoughtfully at
the opposite wall, while his father rose from the bed and
began to busy himself about various household matters,
which might have seemed to an observer almost pathetic
when done by the clumsy fingers of a man. Not that
Guy's fingers were clumsy; they had all the delicacy of a
born musician, and the gentleness of a woman; and it
came quite naturally to him to build up the fire, hang
Tony's flannel pajamas before it, warm some bread and
milk for the child, and finally make and drink a cup of
strong tea before he went back to the orchestra.

"Good-night, Tony. Go to bed soon, there's a good
boy. Shall I unfasten your clothes?"

"No, thank you, Daddy; I'se not a baby," said Tony,
with dignity, and Guy went away laughing at this mani-
festation of infantile pride. He had little to laugh at, and
it was a good thing for him that Tony's smiles and
frowns and baby wiles, as well as the child's innate
genius for music, kept his heart from growing hard. The
amused light was still in his eyes when he reached the
theater, but it would soon have died away had he
known what Tony was doing while he was gone.

"It's a dreat pity," Tony soliloquized as he ate his
bread and milk, when his father's steps had died away,
"it's a dreat pity that Santa Claus doesn't come to poor
little boys as well as rich ones. I s'pose he'll never think
of coming here. But, if I lived in the house where
Daddy used to live, he'd come, because Daddy said if
there were any children there—oh I wish I could go to
Daddy's old house and see Santa Claus for my own self!
What a pity that Daddy doesn't live there now!"

He put away his empty bowl in a little wooden

cupboard, and came slowly back to the fire. Then he yawned, and thought the room looked very lonely, and wondered what he could do to amuse himself. He was a self-reliant little lad, not often in want of occupation, but just now it seemed to him as though something had gone wrong with the world. He was vaguely dissatisfied, and knew not why.

Then a sudden idea occurred to him—one that sent the blood to his cheeks and the sparkle to his eyes. "Tony's ideas" were sometimes a trouble to his father. They were always original, but apt to be impracticable, and even dangerous. The idea that had come to him now was that he should go to the house where his father had lived, and ask to be allowed to wait for Santa Claus when he came down the chimney that night.

"It would be lovely," said Tony to himself. "I shouldn't be no trouble to nobody, and very likely I should be home again before Daddy got back from the theater. I should run all the way, and I should take my fiddle and play 'While shepherds watched,' and sing the words; and then the people of the house would say, 'Oh, there's the waits,'[1] and they would open the front door wide and let me in."

The idea took complete possession of his little soul. As it happened, he knew the name of the house where his father had once lived, and had a general idea of its locality. It was two miles from the big town, but there was an omnibus which would take him almost all the way. And Tony, although kept as closely as possible to his father's side, had a good deal of experience concern-

[1]English carolers.

ing trams, omnibuses, trains, and other modes of transit; and he was not at all dismayed at the notion of making his way to a strange part of the town. He proceeded in haste to make preparations for his expedition. First, he found a piece of paper and scrawled upon it in enormous sprawling letters:

> *Plese, Daddy, I have gone to your old house to find Santerklawse, and I shall tell him to bring things to poor likkle boys as well as ricche ones.*
> *Tony.*

Tony's spelling was not his strong point. Then he put on his cap and his little overcoat, rather thin and very shabby, took his violin under his arm, and so set forth.

The sky was overcast, and the wind cold; but out in the streets the lamps were lighted, the shop windows were resplendent with holly, and a crowd of belated shoppers hustled each other on the pavements, so that Tony, in his delight at this novel and beautiful scene, didn't feel the cold and knew not the meaning of fatigue. At first he even forgot that he meant to go onto a tram and go to Stoneley, the suburb in which his father's home as a child was situated. The name of the house was Carston—as Tony knew; and in his ignorance of all difficulties, he intended to go by tram-car to Stoneley, and then ask the first passerby his way to Carston. That the place might be utterly changed from the time when his father was a boy never even entered Tony's head.

However, the innocent and ignorant sometimes seem guided towards right ways, right things, right people, in ways we do not know. Tony looked up straight into the face of the omnibus conductor at a street corner where several omnibuses were waiting, and said, "Are you going to Stoneley, please?"

And the man looked down at him kindly, and said: "Ay, that I be. Do you want to go to Stoneley, little master?"

"Yes," said Tony, promptly scrambling up the steps, "and I want to go to a house at Stoneley—a house called Carston. Do you know where it is?"

"Why, yes," said the friendly conductor, in rather a doubtful voice. "I know Carston well enough, and we go almost past the gates, but what might you be wanting at Carston, I should like to know?"

"It's where my Daddy used to live," said Tony, settling himself into his seat.

"Oh, I see," said the man, feeling more satisfied. He supposed the boy must be the son of some coachman or gardener who lived at Carston; and Tony had so much self-possession and confidence that no more questions seemed necessary.

More passengers got in, the conductor shouted, the driver cracked his whip, and the omnibus moved on. It seemed a long time to Tony before it stopped to put him down in a dark road, where the conductor pointed encouragingly to a white gate at the end of a little lane, and told him that that was the way to Carston. "There'll be a bus back to town every quarter of an hour," he said; "but maybe you won't want one? You're going to spend Christmas with your father, I reckon?"

"Oh, yes," said Tony, not at all suspecting the drift of the question. And then the omnibus rolled away, leaving him all alone in the dark, with an unaccustomed sensation of fear and—an unusual thing for him—a strong disposition to cry.

But he mastered the weakness, and gripping the violin tighter, he turned towards the white gate at the end of the lane. It was unfastened, and when he had passed through it he found himself on a graveled walk, winding whitely between trees and plantations, towards a large, dark-looking mansion, which Tony divined to be Carston, his father's old home.

He followed the path until he came to the garden, and then he lost himself a little, but by and by he emerged from the shadows, and found that he was facing a wide flight of steps which led up to the terrace in front of the dining-room and drawing-room windows. Tony nodded quite joyfully when he saw the terrace and the steps. His father had told him about them many a time. He mounted them slowly and carefully, then, standing on the terrace, he looked about him a little while and then decided that it was time for him to begin to play. He felt rather cold now that he was not moving, and a snowflake or two melted upon his nose, and made him uncomfortable; nevertheless, it was with great resolution that he drew his bow across the strings of the fiddle, and began his favorite tune—

> *"While shepherds watched their flocks by night,*
> *All seated on the ground."*

"What's that caterwauling in the grounds, Norris?" said the master of the house to the butler, in his crustiest tones. He was at dinner, and the notes of a violin fell strangely upon his ear. "Did I not tell you that I would have no parties of carol-singers this year? They only trample down the plants and destroy the young trees in the plantation. Go out and put a stop to that noise directly."

Norris went out with rather a grave face. It was a troubled one when he returned.

"It's not the carol-singers at all, sir. It's—it's only a little boy."

"Send him away at once, then."

"If you please, sir, he says he wishes to speak to you. I—I think he's a gentleman's son, sir."

"What if he is? He can have no business here. Send him off. Some begging trick, I daresay."

But as the General—for that was the rank of the master of Carston—spoke, the music waxed louder and louder, and a sweet child's voice rang out like a bird's. To the vast surprise of the master and servant alike, the door of the dining-room was pushed open, and there in the hall stood a child with shining hair and big brown eyes, playing and singing, as he had done at first—

> *"While shepherds watched their flocks by night,*
> *All seated on the ground."*

The General's white moustache bristled fiercely, and his voice was harsh and rasping when he spoke.

"Boy—you there! Stop that noise!"

Tony desisted, but turned a look of angelic reproach upon the speaker. "Don't you like it?" he said. "It's my greatest favorite. And you must know it quite well, because Daddy said he used to sing it to you when he was a little boy."

"When he—your father—what do you mean, child?"

"I ain't a child," said Tony, with dignity. "I'm a boy. It's quite a long time since I was a child."

"What's your name?" said the General, listening and smiling in spite of himself. But the answer banished all smile from his face.

"Anthony Liscard Fairfax," said Tony, triumphantly. "Isn't it a beautiful name? It's my grandfather's name, Daddy says. And I haven't never seen him in all my life." And his innocent, trustful eyes looked straight into the face of the very man who was his grandfather.

Norris gasped. He expected an explosion of anger; he almost feared violence. But for a minute or two the General stood perfectly silent. Then he said to the man, "You may go."

"Shall I go, too?" said Tony.

"No. Stand where you are. Now, tell me who told you to come here tonight?"

"Nobody told me. I thinked it for myself."

"Do you see these grapes and sweets?" persisted the General. "You shall have as many of them as you like if you'll let me know who suggested—who put it into your head—to come."

Tony's face grew red. He saw that he was not believed. But he answered gallantly: "I told you—I thinked it for myself. Nobody said one word about coming, and I thinked of it only tonight when Daddy had gone to the theater. He's told me lots of things about this house, and how boo'ful it was."

"So you wanted to see it for yourself?"

"Yes. I wanted to see it, but that wasn't all. Santa Claus comes to this house, don't he?"

Tony pressed eagerly up to the General who seemed not to know how to answer him.

"I can't say. When the children were small—perhaps—"

A vision came to him of himself and his wife, stealing from cot to cot to fill small stockings with toys and sweets in days long passed away. He could not finish his sentence.

"I know!" cried Tony. "Santa Claus always came here when Daddy was a little boy; and when I asked him why he never came to me, Daddy said that he only came to rich children and not to poor little boys like me."

"Are you poor?" said the General, hastily.

"We're not rich," replied Tony, quoting his father, "but we ain't paupers yet. Daddy says so. Who is paupers? I wanted Daddy to tell me, but he had to go to the theater—"

"So he goes and amuses himself, and leaves you with nobody to care for you?"

"It ain't very amusing," said Tony. "It makes him awful tired to play such silly tunes every night in the or–kistra. But he has to do it, or else there wouldn't be no bread and milk for me, nor no baccy for Daddy."

"Where is your mother?" said the General.

The child's face grew grave. "God took her away," he answered, and the General suddenly felt that his old hatred of that singing woman who had beguiled his son into making her his wife was small-minded and despicable. But another notion made him frown.

"So you came here to see what you could get? You wanted Santa Claus's presents?"

"Oh, no, I didn't. I only thinked I'd like to come—'cause Daddy says Santa Claus always came here at Christmas time, and it would be awful nice to see him; but I don't want anything myself. I just want to tell him that there are heaps of little boys much poorer than me, and that if he would go to the poor children it would be much better than going to the rich ones, don't you think so?"

"Well—sometimes," said the General.

"I thought, if you'd let me, I would stop here till quite, quite late," said Tony, confidentially. "I'd wait about till he came, and then I'd speak to him about the poor little boys. Then I'd go home to Daddy. But may I stop here, please, till Santa Claus comes?"

To his surprise, the old gentleman with the white moustache stooped down and took him into his arms. "My dear little boy," he said, "you may stop till Santa Claus comes—certainly; and you may stop forever, if you like."

❄ ❄ ❄

When Guy Fairfax, half distracted by the note which he found on his table, arrived, panting with haste, at Carston that night, he was shown at once into the dining room, where the General sat in his armchair with a child's figure gently cradled on his knee. Tony was fast asleep, and the General would not move to disturb him. He only looked at his son for a moment, and then at the sleeping child.

"Forgive me, Guy," he said at last. "You—and this boy—are all that remain to me. Let him stay—and stay yourself, too, and cheer the last few years of my life. I was wrong—I know I was wrong, but you must come back to me."

And when Tony woke next morning, in a soft white bed and a cozy room, such as he had never seen before, he was a little bit grieved to find that Santa Claus had filled a stocking for him while he'd been fast asleep. But he was quite consoled when his father told him that the old gentleman with the white hair and moustache, who must henceforth be called Grandad, was the best Santa Claus that he had ever seen, and that Tony might go to him after breakfast and sit on his knee while he sang how "shepherds watched their flocks by night," as the Christ Child came with gifts of peace and joy and good will to men.

Adeline Sergeant

Adeline Sergeant wrote for British Commonwealth magazines early in the twentieth century. Little else is known about her today.

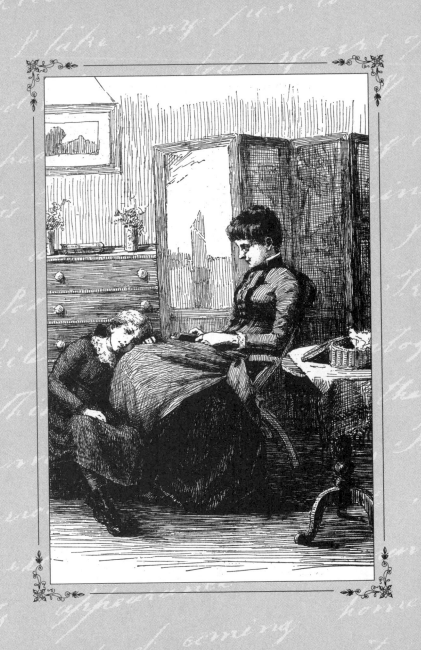

Author Unknown

JOHNNY CHRISTMAS

Pain is an infectious disease. All too often, it blights or kills any who are close to the one experiencing it. So it was with Kate and Tim, after their ten-year-old Johnny died in an icy collision.

Now it was Christmas again—yet the large dark cloud remained, chilling the spirit and killing the dreams.

In desperation, Tim came up with a plan.

❄ ❄ ❄

I firmly believe that this virtually unknown story will one day become one of the most beloved Christmas stories of all. See if you agree.

*K*ate Holloway paused for a moment before a window filled with satin comforters. Pink and blue and yellow. Pale green and gray. The soft lights above brought out their shimmering beauty. A neatly scripted card invited: *Buy a Christmas gift for your home. Only three more shopping days.*

Kate was tall and slim and would have looked younger than her thirty years, except for the harshness about her mouth. She stood in the thin sharp rain and thought savagely, *How can you buy a gift for your home when you have no home? Oh, walls, a roof, a low picket fence, a fireplace. Just a house and a memory.* She stared with bitter eyes at the comforters.

Was it a year ago—or a hundred years—since she and Tim had planned so gaily?

It had been a Christmas lovely to remember. Something for ten-year-old Johnny to have forever. Only he had not lived to hold that memory. Five days later, two days before Tim was to leave for overseas duty, Johnny had been killed. Maybe it wasn't Tim's fault that the car had skidded on the icy pavement, but Kate had wanted Johnny to stay with her. He had begged to go along, and Tim had said with some impatience, "We're only going to drive out to Janey's."

No use thinking about it now. No use remembering the cruel words she had said or the look on Tim's face, the helpless sound of his voice trying to explain. She had not seen him since, but she knew he was back and was living with his sister Janey Lane and her husband. Janey had not forgiven Kate for—as she said—breaking Tim's heart.

Janey had been her best friend when they were in

al and al
ll that s

why did I do
behind her.
possible.
ago.
ing paper
the front
urging
have
very

comforter li
nny would have

omehow she found
she left, there was a bulky
d her bank balance showed
balances were of minor
added to hers each month simply
on living, and work made it
of a small dress shop, she made a
eposited most of it in the bank. There
could buy that would ease the ache

ed on. The rain had turned to sleet that
face and peppered the stiff brown paper under
. The wind swept against her in icy gusts. Up
her white house looked neat and clean—and
inviting. The windows were blank eyes staring at
er. Yet she could not bring herself to leave the house,
because here she felt so close to Johnny.

For the first time in weeks, Kate went into the room
that had been Johnny's, and the pain was almost unbearable when she looked at the smooth bed. At the blue
wallpaper with the band of white ships. The chest of
drawers in one corner and the table where he had
worked on model airplanes. The room was stripped of
his personal things, but his presence was still there.

She put the package on the bed, the comforter spilling out with a gentle whisper. Kate touched it, and then

...t a fool thing to do, and

...e room and closed the door

...re drawn into a straighter line, if

...dn't cry. She'd stopped crying long

...fixed her supper and ate, with the even

...pped up before her, pretending to read. On

...page was an article by the governor of the State

people to take an orphan for the holidays. "Let's

every orphanage empty this year," he said. "Let e

child have a real Christmas."

Kate snorted. What an insane idea! Still, if Johnn

were here—two little boys instead of one romping

about the house. She closed her mind against the im

of Tim.

She remembered a year ago. She had tucked Johnny

into bed, kissed his hard little cheek, and said, "Tomor-

row is Christmas, so you'd better hurry to sleep."

He smiled drowsily and murmured, "That's such a

nice word, Mom. I wouldn't mind if my name was

Johnny Christmas."

She had gone back to the living room where Tim

waited and they heaped the rest of the packages under

the tree. Kate had written on the cards, "To Johnny

Christmas," and laughed when she tied them on his

gifts. He had laughed the next morning when he

opened them.

Kate washed her dishes, hearing above the noise of

running water the sting of sleet needles against the house.

The shivery sound closed her off from the rest of the

world, and magnified her loneliness.

She went to bed early, but not to sleep. She lay there

thinking, and the item in the paper about taking an

orphan child came back to her. She felt vaguely irritated. Surely children like that had a nice time at Christmas. She flounced over and pulled the blanket over her chin. Tomorrow, she decided, she would take the comforter back and send that money to an orphanage. She would send a hundred dollars.

But Kate slept late the next morning and was in a hurry, so she forgot all about it. At noon, she sat at the counter where she ate every day. The girl who waited on her said, "You know, I think that's a swell idea the Governor has."

Kate stirred her coffee and asked in dry irritation, "Wonder how many HE is going to take?"

"Three, the paper says," declared a masculine voice behind her.

Kate's hand froze, and a cold trembling swept her at the sound.

She turned slowly, and there was Tim. He looked the same as always. Older, maybe, than his thirty-five years, and thinner too. His eyes, brown like Johnny's, were remote and the impatience was gone from his face.

"Janey is going to take one," he said, and waited, but Kate ignored his words.

Finally, he said in a kind of despair, "Kate, how long are you going on this way?"

The curve of Kate's lips could not be called a smile. "Why bother, Tim," she said bitterly.

He answered soberly, "Because I happen to love you, Katie. Johnny's loss was my loss too. It broke my heart. And people who love one another should help one another in the dark hours of trial. But I guess I have a life sentence to loneliness."

He paid for his coffee, and walked out, and Kate sat watching his back. She knew it was true. Tim almost went wild at the loss of his child. He stood so lonely, trembling, and she blaming him, and adding to the weight of his anguish and woe. What kind of a woman was she anyway? For a minute, Kate caught a glimpse of her own ugliness, and cruelty. But she swept it aside, being by now so comfortable living with her resentment and revenge.

It was snowing that evening when Kate went home. Huge flakes drifted lazily down, and called "Merry Christmas" to her, though she steeled her heart against it. People all along the street were greeting one another, and the very weariness of their faces was happy. The evening paper carried pictures of children who were being adopted out for the holiday season. Kate hastily turned the page, folded the paper and dropped it on the floor.

She sat before the fire, with her feet thrust out to the flames, eyes half closed, dreaming of seeing on the woolly rug a small boy, with a hurt expression in his eyes. Johnny would not have liked what she'd been doing the past months. He would have said, "Hey, Mom, poor Dad. Why Mom, we're a family . . . no matter what happens. . . . You and Dad . . . then, me. . . ." He would have wondered at her harsh speech, her frowns, and the way she had turned the cold shoulder on her husband, bowed down with grief as much as she. More, for he had her to worry about, besides the anguish at losing a son.

She was relieved when the phone rang. The fingers of accusation were getting pretty close. It was Tim's voice, and though it was brisk and businesslike, it brought an ache to her heart.

"Katie, you've simply got to help me," he said. "Janey was called away to a sick friend, and there is this child coming any minute to spend Christmas. Rick went with Janey, so there's only me. I'll bring the child over and we can talk there."

He hung up before she could protest and Kate went back to sit before the fire and wait. She stirred up her anger. She tried to get furious at the thought of his bringing a child there. "How dare Tim think I could take a strange child, even for an hour," she exclaimed.

She heard a car stop and steps on the walk. She hurried and opened the door before the bell could ring. The snow was falling thickly and it lay on Tim's shoulders and on the shabby coat of the child who stood beside him. A homely little girl with two straw-colored pigtails showing beneath her cap. Tim put his arm about the child, looked directly at Kate, and dared her to deny them entrance.

"This is Johnny," he said.

Kate's fingers tightened on the doorknob. "Girls aren't named that," she said.

The little girl's eyes were wide and brightly brown. "I am," she announced. "Johnny Baker."

Tim brushed the snow from her coat and led her into the clean house. Kate closed the door and followed them.

"Tim," she began, "you know . . . ," but he seemed not to hear. She remembered how stubborn he could be. He was helping Johnny with her coat and presently he was putting her into the brown bed that had held no one for a year.

Kate stood stony-faced, waiting until he came back. "When will Janey return?" she asked.

"I'm not sure," he said slowly.

Kate stared into the fire. She was trembling, and her hands were cold. "This was not kind of you," she said at last. "You could have kept her with you."

"At Christmas," Tim told her, "a child needs a woman. And you, I think, need a child."

"Maybe I do," she said bitterly, "but not just any child."

Tim reached out and caught her elbows tightly in his hands. "I've made you angry, Katie," he said. "At least that's something."

He turned then, and a moment later, she heard the front door close. She was alone in the house, except for a strange child—a girl child—there in Johnny's bed. She went into the room and looked at the small figure humped beneath the covers. The satin comforter lay neatly folded on a chair.

The next morning the little girl stood just inside the kitchen door, watching while Kate made breakfast. "You don't like me, do you?" she asked finally, with the blunt honesty of a child.

Kate smoothed the tablecloth and deposited the pink sugar bowl in the exact center. "Why," she said, confused, "I hardly know you."

"But you don't like me. You don't like anyone." The words were a shock beating against the carefully built up wall. "Only maybe it's not your fault."

Kate was silent, pushing back the feelings of guilt and self-accusation that she knew were all too deserved.

They sat across the table from each other, and Johnny ate oatmeal and drank hot chocolate. Kate noticed there was a sprinkle of freckles across her snub nose, and her wrists were thin. Yet there was something oddly appealing about the little girl. She was like a little chipmunk, watchful, trusting, yet suspicious.

"How old are you?" asked Kate to end the uneasy throbbing silence.

"Ten," Johnny said politely.

Kate took a bite of toast. "Do . . . do . . . you like the Home where you stay?"

"No, ma'am," Johnny was quietly frank. "I hate it. Every one of the kids hate it."

Kate protested. "Why, I thought it was nice."

Johnny's eyes held pity for Kate's ignorance. She lifted her thin shoulders with a shrug. "Oh, it's all right, I guess, if you want to sleep in the same room with fifty other kids, and not have a cat nor nothin'. Only I want a room all my own so I can shut the door and no one can come in 'less I say so!"

She paused and looked thoughtfully at Kate. "Like yours. You got a place for all your things."

Kate changed the subject. "I have to work today. There will be lots of customers. . . . Next-to-the-last-day before Christmas, you know."

The brown eyes across the table glowed. "Oh, that's all right. I like to stay by myself. I'll straighten things up, and cook supper for you."

Kate had thought she would call Tim and have him come and get the child, but somehow she could not dim the eagerness on that small freckled face. All day she worried. *What if the child set fire to the house? Suppose she set fire to herself? Oh, suppose any number of things.* She'd been a fool to leave her alone. Kate hurried home that evening, and paused with one hand on the gate.

She had forgotten that the house could look like that. The windows were warm yellow eyes, inviting her to come in.

Kate's house slippers were by the fire, and in one corner, the radio was turned soft, and was murmuring Christmas carols. The small table in the kitchen was set for two, and there was a cheerful lived-in feeling permeating the entire house.

Kate went into her room, followed by Johnny. The silk comforter was spread on Kate's bed, and Johnny's fingers caressed it. Their thinness hurt Kate's heart.

"It's like a pink cloud, isn't it?" Johnny asked softly. "I didn't think you'd mind if I put it on your bed."

Kate took off her dress and reached for her old housecoat, but Johnny said shyly, "Wear the pretty green one."

Kate touched the quilted fabric. Tim's favorite. She had not worn it since last Christmas. Now she put it on slowly, buttoning it carefully and tying the belt just so.

"It makes your eyes look green," Johnny said in wonder. Tim had said that, too.

They were sitting down to the table when the doorbell rang. Johnny went skipping down the hall to answer it and came back clinging to Tim's hand, her face lifted up to his.

"I've brought candles," Tim announced. "Do I get

invited to eat?" His voice was uncertain. Kate tried to ignore the warmth in his eyes.

"If you like," she said, and Johnny hurried to put on another plate and light the candles.

"They look like Christmas," she said. Then she looked at Kate. "Will we have a tree?" She sounded confident as though she was sure of being there. Kate felt Tim's eyes on her waiting for her answer. Now was the time she ought to tell him to take this little . . . little waif away with him, tonight . . . now. Surely he could find some other place for her. Kate thought she never wanted to see another Christmas tree.

She had the words all planned, but when she looked at Johnny's expectant face, she couldn't say them. "Should we?" she asked.

"It's not Christmas without one," Johnny explained gravely. "I could go on out tonight and get one, if you have to work, or something."

"I don't have to go back," Kate faltered, her tongue playing tricks and saying things she did not intend to say.

"Then, maybe we all can go . . ." Johnny said happily, "like a family."

Kate's fingers tightened on her cup. "I'm sure Mr. Holloway . . . Tim has to work."

"Nonsense," Tim declared loudly. "Even a newspaper guy can get off on Christmas Eve. Especially when he has to buy a Christmas tree."

The next day was cold and clear, with the heady excitement of Christmas riding the wind. The sun turned the crunchy snow into a carpet of diamonds. Johnny hopped along between Kate and Tim. "This is going to be a 'Really' Christmas," she said happily, and shyly tucked her cold fingers inside Kate's gloved hand.

For an instant, Kate held them tightly, remembering the feel of a little boy's hand in hers. Then, she said briskly, "Seems to me you need some gloves."

"I never had any." Johnny was matter-of-fact.

First of all, they bought the gloves, brown leather, fur-lined. Tim's big hands awkwardly smoothed them down on Johnny's hands.

When he had finished, Johnny held them up for Kate's approval. "They are soft and warm and like a nice dream," she said softly, lights shining in her eyes.

The radiance in the child's face put a lump in Kate's throat, and she thought in quick indignation, *Why, every child has a right to things like that . . . they are necessities!*

Then, they had to go and search for a tree that would be exactly right. "Not too tall, not too short, not too fat, not too thin," Tim solemnly explained to Johnny, and she giggled. Kate looked at her, startled to realize that she had not laughed until now. But Tim could always make a child laugh.

Suddenly, Kate could bear it no longer. Planning just as though this were any other happy Christmas, as though nothing had changed. She went home and let Johnny and Tim finish their shopping alone, but the empty house made her restless.

The phone shrilled, and there was Janey's voice—a lot like Tim's—coming over the wire. Janey had not called for a long time. Now she said, "Kate, why don't you come to us for Christmas? You and Tim belong together. You must not continue to blame Tim. What happened was not his fault. It nearly killed him, too."

"I'm sorry, Janey, but you must let me be the judge of that. I suppose you'll want Joh . . . the child this evening." Kate still could not bring herself to say the familiar name. Yet all at once she knew she did not want either the little girl or Tim to go.

"Child?" Janey said blankly. "What on earth are you talking about? I have two orphans here now, and I'm working my idiotic self to death. But we're having more fun than a barrel of monkeys. What child are you talking about, Kate?"

"Oh, never mind," Kate said, and she hung up not long after, still puzzling, and half angry at Tim for deceiving her. What an underhanded thing to do: to foist this child on her, and tell her that Janey was visiting a sick friend! She walked about the house and straightened things with jerky movements. So . . . Janey had been visiting a sick friend, and Tim had to help with a strange child! Kate tried to organize her twisted thoughts for she wanted to be fair, and to understand. But was this fair? Just what was Tim trying to accomplish? She thought she knew.

Still, Kate poked the fire with vicious thrusts, and sparks flew out and disappeared in the chimney. She heard laughter drift up the walk followed by the scrape of shoes on the steps. They came in loaded with packages, and Tim struggling under the weight of the tree that would always be too big. He had always done that. The fragrance of the pine tree spread in a fine cloud through the room.

Johnny hurried to the privacy of the back room to wrap her gifts. Kate stood looking at Tim, her lips tightly drawn, a strange feeling not quite anger surging through her.

"So you know?"

"Yes, I know, Mr. Timothy-Fix-It," she heard her voice say too mockingly. "At Christmas, a child needs a woman."

"I should have taken Janey into my secret," Tim said dryly. "Only she would have felt sorry for Johnny and said this was no place for her on Christmas."

"Maybe she'd have been right," Kate said, sharply. "Maybe you'd better take this waif to Janey right now—and—"

The doorbell interrupted. "That must be Johnny's puppy," Tim said.

Kate forgot her part of the anger. "A *puppy?* She could not possibly keep one at the Home."

The bell rang again, sharp and impatient. Tim turned.

"No," he said, levelly. "But she could keep one here." Amazement kept Kate silent.

Johnny chose that moment to come down the hall, her arms loaded with awkwardly wrapped packages. She deposited them on the nearest chair, and ran to take the puppy in her arms. She didn't go into ecstasies the way some children would have done, but her hands caressed the little dog the way they had the pink comforter: lightly, delicately, lovingly.

The puppy's tongue swiped her cheek. Her eyes were velvet brown come to life. "Will you keep him for me?" she asked Kate. "Will you? And then, maybe I could come and visit you sometime and see him." Again, that crazy lump in Kate's throat. She went quickly into the living room and stood before the fire.

That wall about her heart was threatening to crumble, that wall she had built up against hurt and the whole world.

She heard Johnny ask, "Did I say something wrong?"

And Tim's gentle voice. "No, dear, you didn't. Come on, let's fix the tree." Kate sat in a big, low chair, and tried not to watch. The puppy romped on the floor, and the firelight danced on Johnny's absorbed face, and tangled in her hair. Tim fixed the colored lights, and Johnny turned them on, and then sat back on her heels to admire them.

"Just like a storybook," she said softly. "It is the beautifullest tree there ever was in all the world."

She disappeared and came back a moment later with her hairbrush. She asked Kate shyly, "If I sit on the low stool, will you brush my hair? No one ever did."

Why should words like these sting her eyes with tears, Kate wondered. Her hands were clumsy and the silky strands of hair clung to her fingers like live things. She braided them carefully and tied the ends with bits of ribbon. She suddenly remembered that she hadn't bought a gift for the child. At least she could have done that much! The child was not to blame for Tim's trick, and for the year-long ache in her heart. Johnny curled down on the rug before the fire with the puppy in her arms. She might have been the ghost of Kate's little boy, made feminine and come to life. Johnny tipped her head back to look at Tim.

"The puppy doesn't know that I'm ugly, does he? He likes me just the same as if I'm pretty." Tim looked at her and then across the room to Kate as if to say, *Take over, I have done all I could.*

"Whoever told you a stupid thing like that?" Kate gasped.

Johnny stared into the fire. Her fingers absently scratched the puppy's ear. "Oh, all the girls at the Home," she said calmly. "They say that's why no one ever adopted me. People want pretty children, 'less they are borned to them, and then they don't know the difference, I guess."

Her acceptance of something beyond her control amazed and humbled Kate. For a child as lovely as this to think a thing like that, to have no special corner in all the world for her own. Kate failed to remember that once, so short a time ago, she had thought Johnny homely.

She studied the top of her firelit head.

"How would you like to be adopted by us?" she asked abruptly. The room seemed to hold its breath, waiting. Kate sensed that the last few days had been a prelude to this moment, to the rebirth of the old Kate, long buried beneath a mound of selfishness. She dared not look at Tim.

"You mean," Johnny said breathlessly, in wonder, "we would be a *family*?"

Kate's voice echoed the wonder. "I mean exactly that," she said softly.

Johnny cried then. Huge tears, boiling over and spilling down her face. "I'd be real good," she said, gulping. "I could help you."

Kate bent over and wiped away the tears. "But now," she said gently, "you need to go to bed. Come along and I'll tuck you in."

Kate went first to her room, and gathered up the

comforter, and then came back and spread it on the bed. Tim leaned in the doorway, watching, and she knew with a swift upsurge of happiness that he had seen the miracle of this night. The thread of love was still there, fine and tightly spun, made stronger by the presence of this child.

Johnny climbed between the sheets and smoothed the comforter. "But that is yours," she protested.

"No, it is yours now. From me to you." Kate said. "This is Christmas now, you know."

"That is such a lovely word," Johnny sighed, her eyes already heavy with sleep.

Kate kissed the firm little cheek, as she had kissed another small cheek on other nights.

"A lovely word," she agreed softly. "Now go to sleep, Johnny Christmas."

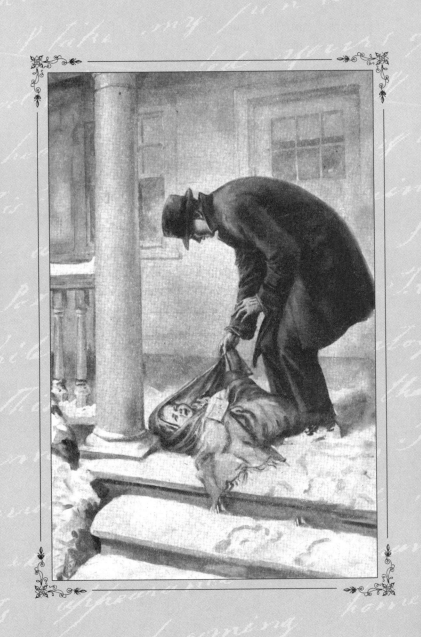

Harriet Lummis Smith

NO ROOM
AT THE INN

It had been snowing hard for some time when Vance reached the porch steps. What was this? "This" was a nine-month-old baby. Obviously, the baby couldn't be left outside in the cold and snow.

Inside, everyone looked at each other in dismay. What should they do with him?

*I*t had been snowing hard since seven o'clock. Vance Merriman, coming up the steps leading to his home, reflected that there would be a job for somebody in the morning. Ordinarily he would have planned to rise early to clear the steps and sidewalk of their snowy covering before breakfast; but Vance, his father, and sister all had jobs, and he resolved to leave this work for some hungry man to whom the snowfall was equivalent to a fall of manna.

As he reached the porch, Vance saw a bundle before him. Some deliveryman, overworked in the Christmas rush, had perhaps failed to ring the bell. This natural explanation ceased to satisfy Vance as he stooped to examine the parcel. It was wrapped not in paper but in a blanket.

A sudden awful suspicion had taken possession of Vance. He touched the bundle gingerly, then lifted the blanket. At once his apprehensions were confirmed by a smothered wail.

Vance inserted his latchkey in the door and opened it. Stooping, he lifted the bundle in his arms. As he reached the hall, he shouted, "Mother!" The whole family answered the summons. His father and mother rushed from the living room! His sister Vivian, addressing Christmas cards in her bedroom, flew down the stairs. Anna, the competent though youthful maid, came hurrying from the kitchen.

"What is it, Vance?" asked Mrs. Merriman. "What has happened?"

"I found this on the porch. I think—somebody left a—baby here."

"A *baby*!" repeated Mrs. Merriman, aghast. "This

winter night?" She took the bundle from her son's arms and the child, disturbed for the second time, began to cry shrilly.

"There's a paper pinned to the blanket," exclaimed Vivian. She carried it to the lamp and read the message aloud.

"He's nine months old, and the best baby, but there doesn't seem to be any room for him anywhere. Please be good to him."

Vance uttered an indignant exclamation. "I'm going to telephone the police station."

"Oh, Vance," cried his mother.

She seemed so shocked that he explained laughingly, "Why, I'm not planning to have the baby arrested, Mother, but the police will know what institution to take him to."

"But surely that's not necessary tonight," said Mrs. Merriman. "Tomorrow I'll telephone the orphanages. The Collier Home would be a good place for him."

As though interested in the discussion of his immediate future, the baby stopped crying. When Mrs. Merriman declared against his resuming his travels that night, he suddenly laughed aloud. There are few sounds more poignant than baby laughter. The Merriman family gasped.

"Well, anyway, he's plucky," said Vance, the first to recover himself.

Anna, who had stood back listening, spoke rather timidly. "If the baby's to stay all night, Mrs. Merriman, I'll keep him with me."

Mrs. Merriman looked at her kindly. "I'm afraid that would be too hard for you, Anna. You're very busy just before Christmas."

"I won't mind it," said the girl eagerly. "I took a lot of care of my little sister, so a baby in the room won't bother me a bit."

Mrs. Merriman drew a breath of relief. "Then I think we'll call that settled," she replied. "Tomorrow I'll devote myself to finding a place for him."

In the morning, when the Merrimans ate their breakfast, they were aware of unwonted sounds in the kitchen: soft coos, shrill squeals, grunts, and gurgles. Anna, deft and prompt as usual, had a half smile on her face as she went between the kitchen and the dining room.

Before they left for their work, Vance and Vivian went into the kitchen to take a farewell look at the baby. He lay on a pillow in a packing box which Anna had requisitioned. At the sight of them, he achieved a toothless smile. Vance gently poked the plump cheek. "Well, old chap, good-by and good luck."

"He's really a pretty little fellow," pronounced Vivian, somewhat surprised.

Vivian was the earliest home that afternoon. When she entered the house, the first sight that met her eyes was her mother with the baby in her arms. "Why, Mother!" cried Vivian reproachfully.

Mrs. Merriman turned. "I've telephoned all over town," she said, "and I can't find a place for this child. This Depression has filled all the Homes to overflowing."

"Then you should have notified the police."

With all the rest of her work, Anna had somehow found time to wash and iron the stranger's little garments. They were of cheap quality but the baby looked fresh and clean. When Mr. Merriman and Vance came in, he set himself at once to interest them: laughing, crowing, and kicking off his shoes.

"Hello! You here?" smiled Vance, although his tone was critical. "Thought I'd said good-by to you for good."

Mrs. Merriman repeated the explanation she had given Vivian, and her son pointed out that the city institutions were under obligation to take charge of an abandoned child. "You'd better have Father do the telephoning," he said. "They won't try to put anything over on him."

"Your mother can attend to that as well as anybody," declared Mr. Merriman hurriedly, and went upstairs.

In the morning Vance and Vivian gave their mother careful instructions as to the best way to get rid of the uninvited guest. After business hours they went downtown to buy a joint present and came home together. As they walked up the steps they heard the baby crying. "Listen to that," said Vance. "The child is still here. The fact is that Mother is too soft-hearted to get rid of him."

They went into the house feeling that the time for firmness had come. Their father and mother were in the living room, and Vance addressed his mother with elaborate sarcasm: "I'm glad you were successful at last in disposing of the baby."

Mrs. Merriman did not pay his satire the tribute of a smile. "Something has come up," she said. "Anna wants to keep him."

"But how could she?" cried Vivian. "Of course she couldn't keep him here."

"That's what she'd like to do."

"It would be interesting, wouldn't it," said Vance feelingly, "to invite some of the fellows in the office home to dinner and have a baby shrieking in the kitchen."

"Yes, or plan a party," said Vivian, "and have the house quarantined for measles."

Mrs. Merriman did not attempt to answer their arguments. She only said, "If we don't agree to it, Anna will leave."

"But where would she go?" asked Vivian indignantly.

"There's a place where they'll take her," replied Mrs. Merriman. "A woman she knows keeps a boarding house on Third Street. I imagine Anna would have to work very hard, but the woman has always wanted her. Today she talked with her over the phone and the woman said she had a child of her own of the same age and that another baby in the house wouldn't make any difference. Anna told her she couldn't come till after Christmas anyway and she'd let her know what we decided."

"I'll have a talk with Anna after dinner," exclaimed Vivian. "Somebody ought to be able to make her see reason."

After the dessert, when the others scattered, Vivian went out into the kitchen. The baby, in his improvised crib, kicked and gurgled at the sight of her. "I came out to have a talk with you, Anna," said Vivian. "I can't imagine why you should want to do anything so silly as keeping the baby. What in the world made you think you wanted to do it?"

On the wall hung a calendar with a brief Bible verse for each day of the year. Anna put her finger on the date on which Vance had found the baby on the porch. "I guess *that's* the reason."

Vivian leaned closer. Slowly and incredulously she read aloud, "There was no room for them in the inn!"

There was a moment of silence and then Anna spoke. "Seems as if it was the same with this child. Mrs. Merriman has been telephoning for two days and they all say they're full up. It scares me to think of taking care of a baby, but somebody's got to find room for him."

"But Anna," gasped Vivian. "That verse means— why, this is different, you see."

"No, I don't see," said Anna, a little stubbornly. "Didn't the Lord Jesus say that what was done for the least of his was done for him? It seems clear to me."

"But you see—" stammered Vivian, and then she paused helplessly. Somehow the conventional arguments did not seem fitted to the occasion. To explain that our obligation to Christ's little ones must be regulated by our convenience, and that no twentieth century Christian went to ridiculous extremes of sacrifice, seemed out of the question. Besides, something in the face of the girl no older than herself gave Vivian a feeling not unlike awe.

Vivian was very silent when she rejoined the family. Perhaps they judged from this that her efforts had been unsuccessful, for at once Vance made a suggestion. "Now listen! I believe this thing will settle itself if we just leave it alone. So I say let things drift for the rest of the month, and I believe Anna will be ready to listen to reason."

"If we're going to have a baby in the house on Christmas, we ought to have a tree," said Vivian.

"I know what ails Vivian," laughed Vance. "She

wants a tree herself and thinks a baby in the house is a good excuse."

Vivian accepted her brother's teasing with a tight-lipped smile. Something in Anna's attitude had changed her feelings about the baby. There was now something terrible in the thought that at Christmas, when the world rejoiced over the birth of a Child, any child should be unwelcome, unwanted.

Christmas Eve arrived and Vance brought home a lovely little spruce which the Merrimans set up in a corner of the living room. The boxes of ornaments had been brought down from the garret and with much laughter they trimmed the tree. The Merriman family still hung up their stockings on Christmas Eve, and when Vivian brought her own, she brought along a pair of tiny blue stockings. "I got a few little things for the baby," she said, defiantly. "So I'm going to hang up his stocking along with the rest."

"Great minds run in the same channel," said Vance, gazing at her with a rather sheepish grin. "But stockings of that size don't hold much, so I'm going to hang mine too."

Vance had bought pink stockings for the baby and a rubber turtle, a rattle that made a prodigious noise, and a woolly dog. As Vivian was exclaiming over the assort-ment, Mrs. Merriman brought out a large package. "I got him a little cap and coat," she said. "It's from your father and me."

The baby entered into the spirit of his first Christmas in a most surprising manner. The Merrimans had been somewhat in doubt as to whether or not he would notice the tree; but when they brought him into the room where it stood radiant, the baby noticed nothing else. He gurgled and laughed. They found it difficult to distract his attention, even by giving him his presents, but the sonorous rattle proved a rival even to the Christmas tree. He sat shaking it joyously.

Anna had not planned to go out on Christmas Day, but Vivian insisted that she should. "Doesn't your church always have something on Christmas night?"

"Yes, but the baby might fuss and bother you. I'd better not leave him."

"I'm going to be home all the evening and I'll look after the baby. So run along and enjoy yourself."

After the baby was in bed and asleep and the usual visitors had gone, Vance noticed his sister busy with a paper and pencil. "Figuring up the cost?" he asked with a grin.

"I'm doing a little calculating," said Vivian, looking up.

The family became attentive. "Three of us are earning," the girl went on. "I was wondering what part of my salary I could put aside to go toward the baby's expenses."

"But, Vivian," exclaimed Mrs. Merriman. "You said—"

"Anna is ready to take care of him," continued Vivian, disregarding the interruption, "and that's all she could do. Then I'll look after him every other Saturday, so Anna can get out, and any evening in the week that she selects."

"Aren't you going ahead rather fast?" demanded Vance. "This house belongs to Father and Mother, you know."

"This is just a hypothetical case. I'm just saying what we could do—IF—I'm not suggesting adopting the baby, understand. But if we should look after him till he's a little older, we might find a good home for him. Of course sometimes it would be hard and inconvenient. But somehow, on Christmas night it seems as if that amounts to very little compared with finding a place for a homeless child."

"As far as I'm concerned," said Vance, "I'm ready to pay my share and do my share. But really Mother is the one to be heard from."

"Me?" exclaimed Mrs. Merriman. She looked at them in vague surprise. "Why, I always wanted to keep him," she said, "from the very first. I thought you understood."

That night before she went to bed, Vivian stole upstairs for a peep at the baby. He was sleeping soundly, his woolly dog beside him. Downstairs the radio was on, and a woman's rich voice was singing *Silent Night*. Looking down at the sleeping child, it was easy for Vivian to believe that He whose birthday they were keeping was glad that one little child, unlike Himself, had a place where he might lay his head.

Harriet Lummis Smith

Harriet Lummis Smith, born in Auburndale, Massachusetts, was a prolific writer of inspirational and value-based stories early in the twentieth century. The author of *Other People's Business*, she also wrote the three books in the *Peggy Raymond* series and the four later books in the *Pollyanna* series (1924–1929). Smith was also the author of a large number of short stories before her death in 1947.

Grace Livingston Hill

STAR OF WONDER

What an opportunity: Beverly had been invited to spend Christmas in a plush New York hotel with her affluent college crowd! Really, it was too good to pass up. Yet, to do so would be to miss Christmas at home. Surely the family would understand—just this once.

*T*he invitation came a week before Christmas and plunged the Whitman household into a whirl of bewilderment. Beverly read it aloud at the breakfast table without realizing what it would contain. (The boys had gone early to school and only her father and mother were there.)

Dear Beverly,

I'm stranded in a New York hotel over Christmas so I'm having a house party. Won't that be great? Besides you I'm asking Floss Everill, Vic Saunders, the Sheldon twins and Violet Fletcher, all our end of college hall.

Of course it's only a hotel, but we have connecting suites and all New York for a playground. Cousin Lew is bringing some of his men friends down from Hartford and there's one particularly stunning young architect I want you to meet.

Now wire me at once what train you'll take and I'll meet you at the Pennsylvania Station. Come not later than Monday afternoon, the twenty-fourth, and Saturday if you can make it. I'm dying to see you again. Don't bother about clothes. Anything will do. You always look nice. And anyway there are the darlingest shops right in the hotel if you should need anything.

Yours for the time of our lives,
Carolyn Kramer

Beverly read more and more slowly, a troubled look coming in her eyes, and there was a dead silence in the room when she finished. Finally her father spoke, a kind of hesitancy in his voice.

"Well, that's certainly kind of her! That will cost them quite a good deal—in a hotel!"

Then her mother spoke in a noncommittal tone.

"She was your roommate at college, wasn't she?" Beverly could see they were both trying to be very polite about it and not intrude in her decision. She experienced a sudden relief that her brothers had left before the mail arrived.

"Yes," she said, glad to be able to answer a commonplace question. "She's a grand girl and very generous. Of course they have loads of money. But she's a dear. These girls she's invited made up our clan. It would be wonderful to see them all." She added wistfully, "It seems like six years instead of six months since we parted at commencement."

There was another silence and then her mother said hesitantly: "You would like to go?"

Beverly cast a quick look at her mother, but she was carefully pouring another cup of coffee for Father and kept her eye on the cup. Her father was thoughtfully crumbling a bit of bread in his fingers. He did not look up either.

"Why, I scarcely know," said Beverly in a troubled tone. "It's such a surprise! Of course it would be nice but I hate to be away from you all at Christmas."

"You mustn't think of us," said her father with forced cheerfulness. "This is an opportunity, of course. You haven't had many. It's always an education to go to New York."

"I'm not out for more education at present," laughed Beverly; "I'm not half using what I've got, you know."

"Well, settle it for yourself, child," said her father,

rising, "I've got to get out and finish that chicken house before we have a snowstorm on our hands."

Father went out and Beverly and her mother began to clear off the breakfast table.

"I'd have to have some new clothes," said Beverly speculatively as she gathered up the silver.

"Not so much," said her mother thoughtfully. "She said not to worry about clothes."

"Yes, but you ought to see her clothes, Mother. She buys a hand-knit dress or two at seventy-five or a hundred dollars apiece and thinks nothing of it."

"Well, you can't compete with that, of course," said her mother with a sigh. "Still, since you're working in the bank, and making your own money, you ought to be able to afford one or two good things. And perhaps your father would feel he could help a little."

"I wouldn't let him!" said Beverly quickly. "Father's got enough financial load with Aunt Lucile in the hospital, and all his money tied up in a closed bank.[2] If I go I'll get what I need myself, but—I had Christmas plans!"

"You mustn't let Christmas plans interfere," said her mother firmly. "You mustn't think of us. We want you to have every advantage. It's a great grief to Father and me that we can't do more for our children."

There was something wistful in her mother's tone that brought the tears to Beverly's eyes.

"Don't, Mother, please!" she said earnestly, flinging her arms about her mother's neck. "We have everything we want. I've had a grand life, Mother, and a wonderful family! I wouldn't have a thing different!"

[2]Story is set during the Great Depression.

"You're a good girl," said her mother, brushing a bright tear away and managing a little trembly smile. "We thank God for our children every day. That's why we want you to accept this invitation—if you really *want* to!"

Beverly gave her mother another quick look. "Why, of course it would be wonderful but—I'm not sure I ought to. Christmas has always been such a very special time with us."

"Well," said her mother with forced cheerfulness, "it's for you to decide, and you mustn't let any thought of us stand in your way. It would be foolish!"

Beverly went slowly, thoughtfully upstairs after the dishes were done, to examine her wardrobe. She would need a new evening dress, and she really ought to have a new winter coat. The old one was terribly shabby. And then—a wool dress of some kind.

Of course she could easily afford to get them if she hadn't ordered those expensive extra Christmas presents for them all, her lovely surprise! They ought to be here today or tomorrow! The new hockey skates and shoes for Stan, the set of books that Graham so longed for, the lovely fur neckpiece for Mother, and the new overcoat for Father. He hadn't had a new one for ten years and wouldn't get one himself. He said he didn't need it yet. But she knew his old one was worn thin and threadbare.

Of course she had other gifts for them, little things that she had made: hemstitched handkerchiefs, neckties, and picture puzzles she had bought some time ago. But these things were special since she got her job. They wouldn't be expected so they could all be returned and nobody the wiser. She could get them again later in the

ɔn when she had earned more money, and they
ɔuld likely be cheaper then. But it wouldn't be like
ɔving them for Christmas!

She turned from the window where she had been
staring out at the drab-brown hills set off by the darker
green of pines on the distant mountains. The sky was
leaden gray and her heart was heavy. She couldn't quite
make up her mind whether she wanted to go to New
York or not.

Her father came in to lunch and said there was a
storm brewing. He warmed his hands at the fire that
snapped cheerfully on the hearth. Oh, home was a
pleasant place! Mother was making mincemeat for the
Christmas pies, and if she went to New York she
wouldn't be here to eat them nor have a part in the
thrill of Christmas morning and the cozy happy time
opening the presents. A pang struck to her heart, but
she told herself crossly that one couldn't be a child
always.

Father went out to his work again, but came back to
get his old sheepskin jacket. He said it was turning bitter
cold and it went to his bones, and Beverly thought of
the new overcoat with another qualm.

She was upstairs looking over her wardrobe again
when the boys came home from school.

"Gee, it's cold," she heard young Stanley say.
"There'll be skating sure for Christmas, but my skates
are too small. Boy, I wish I thought I might get new
ones for Christmas. You don't spose there's any chance,
do you Mother?" he asked wistfully.

"I'm not sure, dear," she heard her mother's troubled
voice. "Your sister has had an invitation to spend

Christmas—" and her voice dropped so that Beverly could not hear the rest. But she heard Stanley's dismayed answer.

"Spend *Christmas*!" he fairly shouted. "You don't mean Beverly would go away from us for *Christmas* do you, Mother? When Graham's going ta make that star and all, and she not here?"

"Hush dear, don't make her feel bad. We mustn't let her know we mind her being away. She doesn't get many chances for a good time."

"Aw, good night! She has as many chances as the rest of us! *I* wouldn't *want* good times if she wasn't in 'em. Not at Christmas anyhow." There were almost tears in the indignant young voice.

"Aw, gee," he went on plaintively, "and we had some surprises for her, too. I've run errands for the grocery every noon for weeks ta get money ta get 'em, and now there won't be any Christmas at all!"

Suddenly Graham's voice broke in upon the dismal wail.

"Who says no Christmas? Sure we're having Christmas! Aren't you and Beverly and I going to surprise—"

Then her mother's voice broke in with a hush. She was telling Graham about the invitation.

"But you don't mean that she's *going*!" broke in the older brother incredulously.

"Why, yes, I think perhaps she should," said her mother sadly.

There was a dead silence below stairs for a minute, then Graham spoke indignantly: "I didn't think Beverly would do a thing like that!" he said furiously. "I thought she—*loved* us!"

out Graham—" her mother's voice protested, and
n the dining room door was shut and Beverly heard
o more. But she did not need to.

She turned back into her room, closed the door, and
sat down in dismay. She hadn't realized how they all
would feel. She had been thinking only about herself.
And now suddenly she realized that she didn't really
want to go at all. She didn't want to be away from the
dear fun and frolic of home. She wanted to see her
mother's face when she wrapped the fur piece about her
neck, to watch the boys when they found their gifts, to
hear Stanley say, "Oh, boy! Hockey skates!" and see
Graham's eyes light up when he discovered the whole
set of books for which he had longed, hidden in different parts of the house as she had planned. She wanted to
sing the carols and sit around the fire while Father read
the Christmas story from the Bible and prayed. She
wanted to help hang up the stockings and trim the tree,
and then steal down when the others weren't looking
and hide the presents where they wouldn't be seen till
morning. There wouldn't be anything like this in New
York. There wouldn't be any atmosphere of holiness,
no thought of Bethlehem among her merry friends.
Christmas was only a holiday to them, a time of giving
expensive gifts and having a good time. And all at once
she knew that if her father and mother knew all about it
they wouldn't think it was such a wonderful opportunity for her either. They were all modern girls, nice,
and good fun, but none of them Christians. She would
be losing Christmas and all that it had always meant to
her, losing it utterly, right out of her year! All at once

Beverly knew that she could not go. That she did not want to go!

She got up quickly and went to her desk to write her telegram.

Sorry but impossible to come. Have made other plans. Many thanks. Love to all. Am writing. Beverly.

Then she put on her old brown beret with the tiny red feather, her old brown coat and warm gloves, and went downstairs.

"I have to go to the village to mail some letters and send a telegram," she called out, opening the dining-room door on the dismayed faces, "who wants to go with me?"

"Why, Beverly, ought you to take time for that? The telegram can be sent over the telephone, and Stanley will take the letters if they must go tonight."

"Time?" said Beverly gaily. "I have plenty of time before I help get supper, unless you need me for something. I thought I'd like a little exercise, and if I telephone my telegram Tilly Watrous will be sure to listen in and broadcast it all over the neighborhood. Besides, the boys and I have some Christmas secrets to talk over and we don't want you spying on us, Mother dear. Graham, how about you taking this telegram over to the office while Stan and I go to the five-and-ten?"

She threw her telegram down on the table. The boys huddled gloomily together and read it without seeming to do so. Her mother gave her a puzzled glance. Then Stanley suddenly cried out with a shout: "She isn't going, Mother! I told ya she wouldn't!"

"Of course she wouldn't!" growled Graham, a great relief in his voice as he pulled on his gloves. "Come on, Kid, I'm with ya!"

The mother glanced at the telegram and then back to her daughter. "Why, Beverly," she said with almost a tremble of joy in her voice, "are you *sure* you want to send that telegram?"

"Yes, I'm *sure!*" said Beverly throwing her arms about her mother's neck and giving her a resounding kiss.

Father came in just then. "It's very cold!" he said with a shiver. He looked blue around his lips. "I think we're going to have a real old-fashioned winter. I hope it won't storm while you're on your way to New York, child!"

"She's not going!" shouted the boys in chorus.

"Now, boys, you haven't been whining around and coaxing her to stay, have you?"

"No, Father," said Beverly, winding her warm young arms about his neck and kissing him on his cold cold nose. "I wouldn't go for anything, not at Christmastime. I wouldn't want to miss Christmas with you all for anybody."

Then they went out for their two-mile walk to the village, gay and full of Christmas plans, and when they came back they had many mysterious packages, and among them were wire and electric sockets and tiny electric bulbs, and strings of lights and silver rain for the tree. They entered their home fairly sparkling with joyous plans, Beverly just as happy as the rest. The spirit of Christmas seemed to have come in with them, and peace and harmony and joy to abide.

All that week they went about with their happy

secrets and there seemed to be among them a sweet intangible something that thrilled the whole family. Even a long, protesting, pleading telegram from Carolyn and finally a lengthy long-distance conversation on the telephone failed to disturb the joy, since Beverly was not going away.

Saturday morning the boys got the tree, a beauty, from their own woods up on the hill a mile away, and set it up in the corner of the big living room.

"It's beginning to snow," said Father as he came in Saturday night from feeding the chickens. "Just lazy flakes but I think it means business."

"Oh, good!" cried Stanley. "A real Christmas!"

It snowed a little at intervals all day Sunday, and when the family drove home from church Sunday night it was three inches deep on the running board and coming down in little fine grains.

"She's off for an old-time blizzard!" said Graham jubilantly. "I thought she was fooling, but I guess she means it!"

Monday morning it was still snowing harder than ever, but the flakes were broad and heavy, big white feathers, piled firmly on top of the hard, grainy foundation. Then the wind arrived and hurled the falling snow into fantastic drifts, heaping it higher and higher every hour, till the drifts were getting so deep they had to make tunnels to the chicken houses and bring some of the chickens into the barn for safety.

"Isn't it lovely!" cried Beverly, pausing in her busy preparations to look out the window. "Look what I would have missed if I had gone away! What fun would there be in a hotel in such weather? They don't have such lovely snow in New York City, I know."

"You dear girl!" said her mother, smiling happily.

"There's a drift ten feet high between here and Harrises," announced Graham coming in from taking a basket of good things to a less fortunate neighbor. "Tom Harris had to go around by Bogg's Corners to get to the village."

"Yes, it's a real blizzard all right," said Father, piling another log on the fire. "I'm glad you're at home, little girl."

"So am I," said Beverly, smiling happily. "Graham, don't you think it would be good to hang that star about an inch lower so it can be seen at night through the arch of the front window?"

"Who's going to see it?" laughed Graham. "There won't be a soul abroad for many a night."

"Somebody might be lost and it would guide them," said Beverly thoughtfully.

❋ ❋ ❋

Gideon Ware climbed stiffly from his car and for the thousandth time that day wiped the heavy coating of snow from his windshield. It lay in great flakes overlapping one another on the glass like frosting on a cake. His windshield wiper was utterly useless. His common sense had told him to get a defroster before he left his home city, but he had started late and was in a hurry at the last to get away from the city, free from business and everything, and he had taken a chance, trusting in his well-proven ability to fight through difficult situations.

Gideon Ware was a big, strong, good-looking young fellow with an attractive manner, a rising business, and just now a lonely bitterness in his heart that made him restless. He hadn't wanted to go to this Christmas affair at the big country estate. He had told the girl who asked him that he would come if he could, but he hadn't meant to go. Yet at the last minute he couldn't stand the thought of Christmas alone in the city, so he had hurriedly purchased a few costly trifles to serve for Christmas gifts if they were in order, and had started, rather craving the long drive through the storm. The journey would have taken him only about five hours in ordinary weather, but it had already been twice that long, and he was not by any means at the end yet if one could judge by the map. He had a horrible fact to face, and that was that he could not now find himself on the map at all. Again and again he had got out and cleaned off a road sign only to read, "Drive slow, School ahead!" or, "New York 90 miles." That didn't help much because he was no longer sure which direction he was coming from. The detours had been most bewildering to his tired brain.

Darkness had descended since he had stopped at the last filling station, and the old man who served him had been vague in his directions.

There had been occasional windswept glares of ice where he skidded around wildly, even with chains. Then he would turn and forge ahead again, wallowing into a dip in the road where the snow lay deceptively deep. He could not follow the line of the fence in the darkness and suddenly the car lurched into a ditch by the roadside. It was more than two hours before he nally got it back again onto the road. His feet were wet, his wrists were wet, there was snow down his neck and up his sleeves. He was nearly frozen. Why had he started on this fool journey? Just because he was tired of plugging away at business with nothing else in life! He didn't especially care for the girl who had invited him. She was pretty and heartless, out to have a good time at any price, like all other girls he knew, but there wasn't anything else to do, so he was on his way, plodding through snowdrifts, not even knowing if he was going in the right direction. Nothing was visible even with his powerful headlights, save this thick blanket of snow through which he was moving. Why hadn't he turned around long ago when there was a place to turn? He could have stayed in his apartment, slept through the day and moped alone. What was a party anyway, and what was Christmas but bunk? An illusion gone that used to make rosy his childhood, when there was a mother and father and home and cheer. He would never see anything like that again.

He was deadly cold and tired. He wished he could drop his head down on the wheel and sleep. His hands and arms were numb. He could scarcely move them they were so cold. People froze to death this way: growing numb, not knowing they were freezing. Well, if he froze to death there was nobody to care!

Was that a light off there to the left or only a mirage, a winter will-o'-the-wisp? It certainly was a blurred brightness, or else he was dying of cold and couldn't discern that it was the light of another world.

And then, as if the car were alive and had seen the light too, it stopped dead in its tracks, stalled, *thump,* with a great white wall looming up ahead, higher than the car, deeper and higher and wider than the universe! The car had buried its nose in the drift and stopped.

He tried to go backward, but the engine just churned away for a minute and stalled again, as if it had given its last breath to save him. He lifted his tired hands that were so heavy and numb and tried to open the door. His feet were aching with cold. The heater had gone dead miles ago and the car had been growing colder ever since.

He managed to get the door open with his numb fingers at last. The world outside seemed terribly still and shut in by that soft white deadly blanket of snow everywhere. What was the use of getting out? It was only colder. There wasn't anywhere to go, and if there was, he couldn't get there. That wasn't a light over there, it was a mirage, and he wasn't Gideon Ware going to a Christmas party, he was just one man freezing to death and it didn't matter. Oh, he was so deadly sleepy. And cold! He would close the door, crawl into the back seat and go to sleep. No one would ever know or care.

It was at that moment that the star blazed out clear and steady. Such a bright star, penetrating that white blanket, able to shine through the window because the house on that side was sheltered from the wind and the snow was driving from the other direction.

A star! And then a sound! Music! Was he dreaming? Could that be angels? Perhaps there was a heaven after all. He didn't belong there, of course. But his mother must be there. She had taught him to pray. Perhaps in assing he might get a chance to speak with her before they sent him away. Hark!

It was only a soft humming at first, several voices tuning in on the melody, just a low humming like wings far away yet somehow strangely familiar. Then they burst out clearly in the white stillness:

> *Oh,—star of wonder, star of night;*
> *Star with royal beauty bright;*
> *Westward leading, still proceeding,*
> *Guide us to Thy perfect light.*

"I'm coming!" called Gideon Ware in an unsteady voice, half to himself. "I'm coming! Don't leave me!"

He stepped down into the snow and fell to his knees, his stiff cold knees, but he struggled up again and the motion woke him to reality. He was waist deep in the snow, wallowing!

Ah! There was a shallower place! He could feel flagging under his foot. He wasn't frozen yet. He would hold out to get to the star! Or was it a house? Maybe it was like traveling after a rainbow, never reaching the pot of gold. But there might be warmth in that star, even if it were but a star, if he could only get there.

With a last struggle he arrived at the door, and fumbling, found the knocker, though it fell from his numb fingers and stopped the music inside, the heavenly music!

"What's that?" said Graham, suddenly rising from the floor where he had been sitting with his back against the wall. "No, Dad, you sit still. I'll go!"

But they all crowded behind him as he flung open the door.

Gideon Ware stood there like a snowman, covered with white from his head to his feet and struggling for words as his mind slowly came back from a white dead world where he had almost slipped away.

"Would you mind—" he said slowly, blinking his snowy lashes, "if I came in for a minute—and got warm—by that star? I think I've been—freezing—to death!"

Strong young arms drew him inside and laid him on the couch. Stanley ran out for a pan of snow to rub on his hands and face, Father put more wood on the fire, Mother went for blankets and towels, and Beverly made some coffee. In a few minutes they had brought him back, all the way back to the room, with the star shining full upon him.

An hour later, warmed and fed and beginning to feel like himself again, Gideon looked about him with his own pleasant grin.

"I must have been pretty far gone, when I saw that star," he said. "I thought this was heaven. And I guess at that I wasn't so far wrong."

"We are certainly thankful God sent you to us before it was too late," said Father heartily. "And now what more can we do for you? Would you like to telephone your friends that you are safe and they needn't worry about you?"

"There isn't a soul in this world worrying about me," said Gideon with another grin. "I was only on my way to a foolish Christmas party that I didn't want to attend.

I would have turned back long ago if there had been a place to turn."

"Well, telephone your Christmas party then that you are going to attend another one instead," said Father. "The roads are practically impassable."

"They are," said Gideon. "I found that out. But I don't need to stay around in your way. Can't I get a mechanic at some garage to tow my car? I can surely make it to a hotel nearby."

"There isn't such a thing nearby," said Graham, "and I can tow your car when it's time for you to go. You can't go till the storm's over, that's a cinch. And as for a mechanic, you couldn't bribe one out here tonight, even if he could get here!"

"You are very welcome here," said Mr. Whitman heartily, "isn't he, Mother?"

"Of course," said Mrs. Whitman with smiling eyes. "We'll be delighted to have a Christmas guest. It will just put the crowning touch to our festivities. Beverly, go make up the guest-room bed."

Gideon saw the welcome in the girl's eyes as she hurried off upstairs and felt more than ever that he had reached at least the vestibule of heaven.

"Now, boys, let's get out and look after that car so nobody else will run into it in the night," said Mr. Whitman, bringing out his old sheepskin coat and cap and mittens.

"Indeed, you will not," said Gideon springing up, "I'm entirely able to do anything that has to be done."

"Now, Son, lie still," said Father, putting a firm hand on his arm. "You would catch your death of cold after the steaming we've given you. The boys will count it a privilege, a joke!"

Gideon finally succumbed to the Whitman determination, and felt like a big child, sitting wrapped in blankets, in the armchair beside the fire.

Outside the boys were working with snow shovels and whistling Christmas carols. Beverly's voice from above sounded softly in tune with them, humming as she worked. It seemed a blessed place into which his lines had fallen. And presently he heard the *chug-chug* of a flivver backing out of the old barn and coming to rescue its aristocratic brother from the drift. A strange sweet lassitude of blessed comfort and rest settled down over the guest.

"Now," said Father a little later, as they came stamping in, shaking the snow from their garments, "we must get this man to bed at once!"

"We must hang up our stockings first!" cried Stanley. "Can't I get one of Father's socks for Mr. Ware, Mother?"

"Of course," said Mother smiling. "Here, I'll get one."

"Oh, please don't bother about me," begged Gideon, "I haven't hung up a stocking since I was a kid."

"All the more reason why you should now," said Father. "There are plenty of apples and nuts and maple-sugar hearts to put in it," he laughed.

"You are very kind," said Gideon, deeply touched.

When the stockings were hung they all settled down quietly as Father took up the Bible and read the Christmas story of the star of long ago. Beverly was seated on a low stool by the fire and Gideon watched the firelight playing over her sweet face and wondered at himself that he should be there. Then the father prayed, not forgetting "the stranger within our gates," that he might have great blessing, and thanking the Lord "for saving him from the deadly peril of the storm." That prayer somehow made Gideon ashamed of his indifference and unbelief, and hardness of heart and gloom. If there were people like these in the world, a home like this, and a girl like that one over by the fire, life must be somehow worthwhile after all.

Up in the quiet of the guest room he searched his suitcase for the Christmas packages he had bought so indifferently for those other strangers. He swept aside the gold cigarette cases and jeweled vanity cases and bridge sets, but there was a pin he had liked, a delicate thing of amethysts and pearls that would do for the sweet mother, and there was a bracelet, a slender hoop of platinum set with emeralds and tiny diamonds. Would the girl like that?

There was a handsome silk muffler for the father, and a pair of cuff links and fur-lined gloves that would do for the boys. He got into the big lavender-scented bed well satisfied, and fell asleep at once.

There were buckwheat cakes and homemade sausage for breakfast. Gideon thought he had never tasted anything so good. There was a brief happy worship again at the table, and then they all adjourned to the living room around the fire to open the presents.

Gideon was taken right into the circle as if he belonged, and he entered into the spirit of the day as if he had always been having such Christmases.

His stocking was bulging, and there was a bag of butternuts and another of apples, down on the hearth

underneath it. There was a pair of fine woollen socks that
Mother had knit, a handsome compass from Graham that
he had won as a prize in a school contest and treasured
greatly, a trick flashlight that Stanley had saved pennies for
months to buy for himself, and down in the toe of the
stocking a small exquisitely bound Testament in dark blue
leather and gold, one of Beverly's recently acquired treasures. She had written in it, *Christmas Greetings to Mr.
Ware from Beverly Whitman,* and been a little troubled lest
he should be offended at such a gift, as if she thought he
had no Bible. Yet she had nothing else suitable to give.

But the look he flashed across the room to her when
he opened it, and the smile that went with the look,
showed that he liked it.

Gideon entered into everything all day as if he were
one of the family. He watched the stuffing of the turkey,
and even helped Beverly to set the table; and later in that
wonderful day when the big brown turkey had been
eaten, with all its accompanying vegetables and cranber-
ries and mince pie and the like, and more carols had been
sung, the sun shot out for a while. Then they all issued
forth into the white wonderful world and shoveled paths
and made snowballs, and a marvelous snowman.

When the dusk came down and they came in, there
was the firelight and the star gleaming. Gideon and
Beverly stood together by the big arched window and
looked at the star for a moment silently. They were
alone, for the rest of the family were busy about some
household matters.

"I shall always be grateful to that star," said Gideon in a
low voice, his face lifted thoughtfully to its soft shining.

"It not only saved my life," he suddenly looked down into the girl's sweet eyes, "but—it—led me—to *you!*"

He hesitated just an instant, and added in a solemn tone as if he meant it with all his heart: "And I think it has started me—on the way back to God!"

He put out his hand and laid it over the girl's, and Beverly, not drawing hers away, looked up with a joyous light in her eyes.

"Oh, I'm glad!" she breathed softly. "Then you didn't mind my giving you the Testament?"

"I loved it!" he said solemnly.

After a moment, his hand still over hers, he spoke again. "I have never seen a girl like you, Beverly. May I come again soon to see you?"

The look she gave him as she said quietly, "I wish you would," bespoke a warm welcome for him when he came.

Late that night, up in her own room alone, she said as she knelt down to thank God for the blessings of the day, "And oh, suppose I had gone to New York instead of staying at home! I'm so glad God showed me in time before I went off on my own selfish way."

Grace Livingston Hill

Grace Livingston Hill (1865–1947) was born in Wellsville, New York, and lived most of her life in Swarthmore, Pennsylvania. A prolific columnist, short-story writer, and novelist, she is significant for yet another reason: her works, emphasizing Judeo-Christian values, have remained popular and in print for more than half a century now.

Anna Brownell Dunaway

GOOD OLD CHRISTMAS PREFERRED

One after another, Beth, Faye, Ned, Father, and Mother all voted for a new kind of Christmas: instead of receiving unwanted gifts, each would buy his or her own gifts, thereby being assured of Christmas happiness. But, along the way, there was a glitch or two . . . or . . .

*O*h, my friends and oh, my foes, if any," Beth
Royden announced airily at the breakfast table, "I
make a motion that we do away with the annual shopping orgy and have a Reformed Christmas."

"I'm for reform, all right," seconded her sophomore
brother, Ned. "I've got a dozen ties that I can't even
work off on the janitor's boy. I gave him one of 'em last
Christmas, but I've never caught him with it on."

"That's just it," Beth said briskly. "Personally, I've
had enough of this Christmas Common. It's simply
absurd having people give you things you don't need
and don't want and don't like. I move that this year we
invest in Christmas Preferred."

"Who's talking about stocks and bonds?" demanded
Faye, Beth's high school sister. "Beth would commercial-
ize Christmas just because she works in a broker's office.
If you mean that nobody's going to get any presents—"

Beth interrupted her impatiently. "Don't be silly,
nitwit. Of course we'll get presents. Wait until I explain
my new and improved Christmas scheme. We shall each
of us decide what we can afford to spend for presents for
each other. And we'll take that money and buy things for
ourselves instead. In that way we won't get impossible
ties and imported pigskin spur cases and whatever. And
we won't have to be hypocrites and all that sort of thing."

"Now that I see the light," Faye capitulated, "I think
that's a perfectly good idea. Last year I wanted a silk
negligee, and what did I get? *Alice in Wonderland* and a
couple of gadgets."

Mr. Royden looked up from the sport page and
laughed appreciatively. "Sounds like a sensible scheme

to me," he approved. "I never do know what to give anybody. Count me in on Christmas Preferred."

"Any further discussion?" Beth inquired, with businesslike efficiency. "What about you, Mother?"

Mrs. Royden smiled thoughtfully from behind the coffee urn. "I am almost sold on the idea myself," she said. "I never get the things I really need. Last year my sheets were down to six, and my tablecloths were threadbare, and I needed kitchen pots and a bathroom rug." She laughed ruefully. "But I got a cut-glass vase and a pair of modernistic bookends and an atomizer. Not that I didn't love them, of course."

"There!" cried Beth triumphantly. "The old, hypocritical, loving fib, 'Oh, it's just what I wanted!' "

"Well, I know what I want and what I'm going to get," Faye declared, "as soon as I collect the family filthy lucre. It's a whole outfit—brown dress, hat, gloves, shoes and scarf. I know I might take you all window shopping, but you'd never remember. You'd give me a whole hodgepodge of colors like Joseph's coat—"

"And I'll get myself a nine-tube radio for my room," Ned chortled. "Good-by, military brushes, and green neckties, farewell."

"Carried unanimously," Beth said, with dispatch. She drew a pencil from her bag and addressed her father. "Dad, about how much did you count on spending for our Christmas presents this year?"

"Eh? What's that?" Mr. Royden blinked a little at the suddenness of the onslaught. "Er—let me see." He usually did his shopping the last minute, buying recklessly from depreciated stocks. "Well, last year I spent fifty dollars. But with two salary cuts—"[3] He cleared his throat nervously under the barrage of eyes. "Make it twenty," he said finally. "About five dollars apiece."

"Fine," Beth said approvingly. She poised her pencil expectantly. "Mother?"

"Mine, you know, Beth," Mrs. Royden answered, a note of apology in her voice, "will have to be what I can spare out of the household budget. And there must be some, too, for the Salvation Army kettles and the Good Fellows. But I think I can squeeze out about four dollars apiece." She flung out her hands deprecatingly. "Without the secrecy and all, it sounds sort of crude and commercial, I'm afraid. I wish I could give you each a check for a million if it's to be a money Christmas."

"Money Christmas, nothing!" Beth exclaimed. "We're investing in gilt-edged Christmas Preferred. We're doing away with mush and sentiment and insincerity and all that racket. Well, Ned, you're next."

"Ten's my figure," Ned declared. "No more, no less. Take it or leave it."

"Is this an auction or not?" Faye demanded.

"Unsentimentally speaking," Ned grinned, "my exchequer is limited. With only a part-time job—"

"It's perfectly all right, Neddy. We understand," Beth cut in soothingly. "Two and a half apiece for you. Next, Faye."

"Well, let me see," Faye considered, wrinkling her small nose, "owing to the cares of this life and the deceitfulness of riches, I think two apiece is my absolute

[3]This story was set during the Great Depression, when those who still had jobs experienced one salary cut after another.

limit. What with my allowance being cut, and car fare and lunches—"

"Eight dollars," Beth said matter-of-factly. "All right. As for me, I was going to spend five dollars apiece on you two"—she nodded at Ned and Faye—"and split fifteen on Dad and Mother. Let me see, that gives each of us enough to buy a really respectable present. Around sixteen dollars apiece."

"Sixteen-fifty for me," announced Faye gleefully. "And that will give me a brown outfit with what I put with it!"

"My radio, my radio," Ned parodied.

"Looks like an emancipated Christmas," beamed Mr. Royden. "I'll get that set of books I've been wanting."

"Six new sheets," Mrs. Royden murmured abstractedly, "a dozen towels, an oil mop—why, think of the things I can buy with sixteen dollars!"

"Seventeen for you, Mother," Beth corrected, as she made a hurried rush for her car.

All the way down to the loop, her mind revolved happily around a certain pearl tiara with earrings to match, which she had seen in a jeweler's window on State Street.

"Only last year," she mused, "I gave Dad that brocaded lounging robe, and he just lives in his old house jacket. And there was that five-dollar tie I gave Ned. It's time the whole world reformed."

At noon Beth broached the subject to the young junior partner of the firm, who had asked her to lunch. She was so happy over the new scheme that she felt like shouting it from the housetops. When she mentioned, however, that their family was investing in Christmas

Preferred this year instead of Christmas Common,
Randall Harper seemed unimpressed.

"Christmas Preferred?" he repeated, puzzled.

"Yes. We're absolutely through with Christmas
Common—the old-fashioned giving of useless presents.
We've decided that selecting anything for another
person to wear is simply impertinent. So we're collecting the money in advance from each other and buying
what we want."

"I see. In other words, buying yourselves presents."

"Why, of course, if you want to put it that way,"
Beth said, flushing.

"It's a very clever idea," he said slowly, "but I
wonder if we're coming to that in this machine age.
Seems to me like a festival of selfishness. Where is the
Christmas spirit?"

"Dead," Beth answered gaily. "Dead as Marley's
ghost. There isn't any such animal."

As they waited for their order in the smart little
restaurant, the air was suddenly filled with a familiar
melody. Over the radio a tenor voice was singing a
Christmas carol:

> *How silently, how silently,*
> *The wondrous gift is given!*
> *So God imparts to human hearts*
> *The blessings of his heaven.*

"No, Beth, the Christmas spirit is not dead," Randall
said softly. "It lives in that song. I may be old-fashioned,
but it takes me back to Christmas back home when I
was a boy. Doesn't it you?"

Beth nodded without speaking. The haunting music was carrying her back to a vanished year, to the memory of Christmas-green spelling *Peace on Earth*; to a fireplace hung with holly.

"I've made out my list," Randall observed, over the dessert. "I'm afraid I'm too benighted to adopt your clever scheme. Just old associations, maybe, and force of habit and memories and that sort of thing." He leaned toward her eagerly. "I'm doing my Christmas shopping Saturday afternoon. You couldn't—er—"

Beth rose precipitately. No, not on her life could she spend Saturday afternoon shopping with a man. No, indeed. She was emancipated.

Two days before Christmas the Royden tree was set up and trimmed. It was a pretty tree, glittering with the usual icicles, tinsel, ornaments and lights. Somehow the well-remembered fun and spontaneity were missing.

"Looks like we might have saved the expense," Father said.

"But then it wouldn't seem like Christmas at all," Mother reminded him a little sadly. "Why, it would be unthinkable."

"I don't believe I'll even go to the trouble of wrapping my outfit," Faye declared, without interest. "It's sort of pointless to pick out spiffy wrapping paper and seals and tags just to do up something for yourself."

"But you must," Beth insisted, trying to bring back something of the thrill of those Christmases when she had lain awake listening for the reindeer. "You've got to pretend it's mysterious, if it isn't."

"Oh, yeah?" Ned scoffed, with brotherly candor. "Who's hypocritical now?"

On Saturday afternoon, Beth mingled with the
throng of shoppers on State Street, trying to compare
prices on tiaras. Somehow the one in the jeweler's
window was disappointing, or was it that her interest in
tiaras was waning, now that one was practically within
her grasp?

The holiday atmosphere at Field's almost took her
breath away. In spite of herself, Beth thrilled to the intangible spirit of giving. She found herself saying, "How
Faye would love that," or, "That's the very thing for
Mother." Suddenly she stopped before a booth of shining
glass—goblets, tumblers, sherbets, etched in dazzling
flower designs. As she stood lost in admiration, the
thought struck her that they were down to five matched
tumblers. Her mother had always loved beautiful things—

"I'll take a dozen of these," she said to the clerk, and
then remembered tardily their Christmas Preferred pact.

"Ten dollars," said the salesgirl.

Beth slowly unfastened her purse and then determinedly extended a bill.

I don't care, she said to herself defiantly. *Mother never
would buy them for herself. Oh, bother the old tiara!*

I suppose I'm silly, absolutely maudlin, she laughed. *And
now for cuff links for Ned.* Over the jewelry counter she
ran into Randall. His eyes brightened when he saw her.

"Maybe you can tell me what to get Mother," he
said. "I gave her a brooch last year and the year before
that. She must have a dozen—"

Beth fairly dragged him over to the sparkling booth of
crystal. He bought a set each of goblets and sherbets and
left directions to have them packed and sent as a gift.

"And is that a load off my mind," he said gratefully.

"You're a regular fairy godmother, and you don't believe in Christmas Common either."

"Yes, I do!" Beth cried. "I found out that Christmas presents aren't things at all. They are *thoughts*."

"Great!" he beamed, relieving her of the packages with which she was hung. "You look like Mrs. —I should say Miss—Santa Claus. I see that I'll have to take you home." At the door he tucked a tiny white package into her hand.

"Not to be opened until Christmas," he said, his voice very low.

Her cheeks as red as holly berries, Beth rushed into the house. Her mother was disposing packages around the tree.

"I just couldn't bear to spend all that money on myself," she confessed guiltily. "I hope you won't mind, Beth." A clatter of heels came down the stairs.

"Here I come like the Greeks bearing gifts," cried Faye. "I've been tying 'em up. Will you both kindly clear out while I put my presents on? No, they're not for me, if you must know it. Just as if I wanted an old Christmas Preferred. And if you don't like it, Beth, you can lump it."

Beth dropped into a chair with a peal of laughter.

"*Et tu, Brute!*" she said, when she could speak. "Well—"

The sound of a key turning surreptitiously in the lock was heard and Mr. Royden entered, loaded with bundles. He looked at them with a deprecating air.

"Just a few little—er—knickknacks," he stammered. "Couldn't help it. Force of habit, I guess. You're all right in theory, Beth—"

"As a family," Beth interrupted him, "we're a wash-out. What about that set of books?"

"Oh, that? Well, to tell the truth, it seemed silly to buy books when the shelves won't hold what we have." He came over to Beth and whispered behind his hand. "I got Mother a *lavallière*—coral."

Beth squeezed his arm. At that moment, the door burst open violently.

"Gangway!" Ned shouted. "Vamoose!" He stood glaring at them, his pockets bulging, his hands behind him. "This is a free country, isn't it?" he demanded of Beth. "A fellow can go Christmas Common if he wants to, can't he? Well, that's what I did, believe it or not—"

"But your radio, Ned," Beth cut in, fairly bursting with mirth.

"Who cares for a radio? I was just joking. Anyway— well, I sort of wanted to recapture the old Christmas spirit I had when I was a child and bought Mother a chocolate mouse with my first dime. And while I'm about it, I might as well tell you that those neckties were just what I wanted too, no jokin'."

"Neddy." Beth, looking at him, with an odd little feeling in her throat, saw that he really meant it too. "I guess we're all just as old-fashioned as anything. We just naturally had to invest in good old Christmas Common after all!"

Anna Brownell Dunaway

Anna Brownell Dunaway wrote greeting-card messages, short stories, and at least one book. Little is known about her today.

Thomas J. Burns

THE SECOND GREATEST
CHRISTMAS STORY EVER TOLD

Sales of his last novel had been considerably less than expected, hence his publisher threatened to reduce future advances. His expenses were enormous. What if his career had peaked and it would be all downhill from there?

Bleak childhood memories engulfed him. Was he doomed to repeat his father's terrible fate?

❄ ❄ ❄

From its first publication, A Christmas Carol *has charmed and inspired millions. There have been scores of editions and translations, and many stage, TV,* and film adaptations, making it one of the best-loved stories of all time. Less well known is the fact that this little book of celebration grew out of a dark period in the author's career—and, in some ways, changed the course of his life forever.

*O*n an early October evening in 1843, Charles Dickens stepped from the brick-and-stone portico of his home near Regent's Park in London. The cool air of dusk was a relief from the day's unseasonal humidity, as the author began his nightly walk through what he called "the black streets" of the city.

A handsome man with flowing brown hair and normally sparkling eyes, Dickens was deeply troubled. The thirty-one-year-old father of four had thought he was at the peak of his career. *The Pickwick Papers*, *Oliver Twist* and *Nicholas Nickleby* had all been popular; and *Martin Chuzzlewit*, which he considered his finest novel yet, was being published in monthly installments. But now, the celebrated writer was facing serious financial problems.

Some months earlier, his publisher had revealed that sales of the new novel were not what had been expected, and it might be necessary to sharply reduce Dickens' monthly advances against future sales.

The news stunned the author. It seemed his talent was being questioned. Memories of his childhood poverty resurfaced. Dickens was supporting a large extended family, and his expenses were already nearly more than he could handle. His father and brothers were pleading for loans. His wife, Kate, was expecting their fifth child.

All summer long, Dickens worried about his mounting bills, especially the large mortgage that he owed on his house. He spent time at a seaside resort, where he had trouble sleeping, and walked the cliffs for hours. He knew that he needed an idea that would earn him a large sum of money, and he needed that idea quickly. But in his depression, Dickens was finding it difficult to write. After returning to London, he hoped that resuming his nightly walks would help spark his imagination.

❋ ❋ ❋

The yellow glow from the flickering gas lamps lit his way through London's better neighborhoods. Then, gradually, as he neared the Thames River, only the dull light from tenement windows illuminated the streets, now litter-strewn and lined with open sewers. The elegant ladies and well-dressed gentlemen of Dickens' neighborhood were replaced by bawdy streetwalkers, pickpockets, footpads and beggars.

The dismal scene reminded him of the nightmare that often troubled his sleep: A twelve-year-old boy sits at a worktable piled high with pots of black boot paste. For twelve hours a day, six days a week, he attaches labels on the endless stream of pots to earn the six shillings that will keep him alive.

The boy in the dream looks through the rotting warehouse floor into the cellar, where swarms of rats scurry about. Then he raises his eyes to the dirt-streaked window, dripping with condensation from London's wintry weather. The light is fading now, along with the boy's young hopes. His father is in debtors' prison, and the youngster is receiving only an hour of school lessons during his dinner break at the warehouse. He feels helpless, abandoned. There may never be celebration, joy or hope again. . . .

This was no scene from the author's imagination. It was a period from his early life. Fortunately, Dickens' father had inherited some money, enabling him to pay off his debts and get out of prison—and his young son escaped a dreary fate.

Now the fear of being unable to pay his own debts haunted Dickens. Wearily, he started home from his long walk, no closer to an idea for the "cheerful, glowing" tale he wanted to tell than he'd been when he started out.

However, as he neared home, he felt the sudden flash of inspiration. What about a Christmas story! He would write one for the very people he passed on the black streets of London. People who lived and struggled with the same fears and longings he had known, people who hungered for a bit of cheer and hope.

But Christmas was less than three months away! How could he manage so great a task in so brief a time? The book would have to be short, certainly not a full novel. It would have to be finished by the end of November to be printed and distributed in time for Christmas sales. For speed, he struck on the idea of adapting a Christmas-goblin story from a chapter in *The Pickwick Papers*.

He would fill the story with the scenes and characters his readers loved. There would be a small, sickly child; his honest but ineffectual father; and, at the center of the piece, a selfish villain, an old man with a pointed nose and shriveled cheeks.

As the mild days of October gave way to a cool November, the manuscript grew, page by page, and the story took life. The basic plot was simple enough for children to understand, but evoked themes that would conjure up warm memories and emotions in an adult's heart. After retiring alone to his cold, barren apartment on Christmas Eve, Ebenezer Scrooge, a miserly London businessman, is visited by the spirit of his dead partner, Jacob Marley. Doomed by his greed and insensitivity to his fellow man when alive, Marley's ghost wanders the world in chains forged of his own indifference. He warns Scrooge that he must change, or suffer the same fate. The ghosts of Christmas Past, Christmas Present and Christmas Yet to Come appear and show Scrooge poignant scenes from his life and what will occur if he doesn't mend his ways. Filled with remorse, Scrooge renounces his former selfishness and becomes a kind, generous, loving person who has learned the true spirit of Christmas.

❋ ❋ ❋

Gradually, in the course of his writing, something surprising happened to Dickens. What had begun as a desperate, calculated plan to rescue himself from debt— "a little scheme," as he described it—soon began to work a change in the author. As he wrote about the kind of Christmas he loved—joyous family parties with clusters of mistletoe hanging from the ceiling; cheerful carols, games, dances and gifts; delicious feasts of roast goose, plum pudding, fresh breads, all enjoyed in front of a blazing yule log—the joy of the season he cherished began to alleviate his depression.

A Christmas Carol captured his heart and soul. It became a labor of love. Every time he dipped his quill pen into his ink, the characters seemed magically to take life: Tiny Tim with his crutches, Scrooge cowering in fear before the ghosts, Bob Cratchit drinking Christmas cheer in the face of poverty.

Each morning, Dickens grew excited and impatient to begin the day's work. "I was very much affected by the little book," he later wrote a newspaperman, and was "reluctant to lay it aside for a moment." A friend and Dickens' future biographer, John Forster, took note of the "strange mastery" the story held over the author. Dickens told a professor in America how, when writing, he "wept, and laughed, and wept again." Dickens even took charge of the design of the book, deciding on a gold-stamped cover, a red-and-green title page with colored endpapers, and four hand-colored etchings and four engraved wood-cuts. To make the book affordable to the widest audience possible, he priced it at only five shillings.

At last, on December 2, he was finished, and the manuscript went to the printers. On December 17, the author's copies were delivered, and Dickens was delighted. He had never doubted that *A Christmas Carol* would be popular. But neither he nor his publisher was ready for the overwhelming response that came. The first edition of six thousand copies sold out by Christmas Eve, and as the little book's heartwarming message spread, Dickens later recalled, he received "by every post, all manner of strangers writing all manner of letters about their homes and hearths, and how the *Carol* is read aloud there, and kept on a very little shelf by itself." Novelist William Makepeace Thackeray said of the *Carol*: "It seems to me a national benefit, and to every man or woman who reads it a personal kindness."

Despite the book's public acclaim, it did not turn into the immediate financial success that Dickens had hoped for, because of the quality production he demanded and the low price he placed on the book. Nevertheless, he made enough money from it to scrape by, and *A Christmas Carol*'s enormous popularity revived his audience for subsequent novels, while giving a fresh, new direction to his life and career.

Although Dickens would write many other well-received and financially profitable books—*David Copperfield, A Tale of Two Cities, Great Expectations*—nothing would ever quite equal the soul-satisfying joy he derived from his universally loved little novel. In time, some would call him the Apostle of Christmas. And, at his death in 1870, a poor child in London was heard to ask: "Dickens dead? Then will Father Christmas die too?"

In a very real sense, Dickens popularized many aspects of the Christmas we celebrate today, including great family gatherings, seasonal drinks and dishes and gift giving. Even our language has been enriched by the tale. Who has not known a "Scrooge," or uttered "Bah! Humbug!" when feeling irritated or disbelieving. And the phrase "Merry Christmas!" gained wider usage after the story appeared.

In the midst of self-doubt and confusion, a man sometimes does his best work. From the storm of tribulation comes a gift. For Charles Dickens, a little Christmas novel brought newfound faith in himself and in the redemptive joy of the season.

Thomas J. Burns

Thomas J. Burns is a contemporary freelance writer.

Margaret E. Sangster, Jr.

THE TREE IN
THE WINDOW

---

*Clare was lonely, and the vast city was so impersonal.
And now it was lonelier still, for Christmas was
coming. But Clare decided to at least put up her tree
in her one window—city or no city!*

Clare Kimball was trimming her Christmas tree.
Despite the fact that she was alone, she told herself,
she should have a tree, and the prettiest tree in the whole
city! Of course, trees—she paused for a moment to brush
a telltale drop of moisture from her eyes—went with
families, and she had not any family; she had not even a
pretend family. That, however, need not keep her from
hanging tinsel, colored globes and gilt stars on the green
branches of evergreen!

The tree was not a very large one, but it was beautifully proportioned. Its lower branches were wide-
spreading and fuzzy; it tapered not too sharply toward
the slender top. It was the right height to stand in the
window of her combination kitchen-living-room-and-
bedroom. It filled the whole of her one window, from
the top to the bottom. Clare, trimming it, made believe
that the people across the street knew her and were
watching her. She made believe that she was back in
the country where real neighbors were interested in the
things she did. She realized the spirit of Christmas
would be dimmed if she kept remembering that the
house across the way was an impersonal apartment
house.

Clare had been in the city for a month and she had
hardly spoken to anyone except the staff of her office, the
owner of the neighborhood delicatessen, the pastor of the
great stone church on the corner, and an old gentleman
who had shared with her a pew in that church. Her
casual observation was that the younger generation of city
dwellers moved in fast-closed cliques; they did not gather
in the warm-hearted fashion of the rural districts. The
girls in the office had their families, their beaux and their

intimate friends. The young men in the office were mostly either married or engaged—and, anyway, none of them was particularly attractive to Clare. In fact, since she had been in the city, she had seen just one man who had caught her imagination. As she trimmed her tree, she thought of him and smiled mistily. She did not know his name; she simply remembered that she had seen him quite often on the street, and once he had gotten up in a trolley car to give her his seat. She knew, because of the frequency of these meetings, that he probably lived in the neighborhood, and she knew also that he had the nicest smile and the deepest blue eyes and the reddest, reddest hair! That was the most she did know—and, she reminded herself, sternly, it was probably all she ever would know. The red-haired man was romantic, but from a distance. Romance, Clare had observed, was always viewed from a distance in her case.

This was unfortunately quite true, for despite the fact that Clare was pretty, she had not experienced very much in the way of excitement and thrill in her twenty-one years. From the time she had been old enough to go places and do things, she had been held fast to her home. She had spent her young days in taking care of a house, in making beds, washing dishes, and baking bread and pies—filling the place of the mother that she had known only fleetingly as a pale and silent invalid. When her father had died a few months before, she had settled the affairs of the aforementioned house, had, in fact, sold it with the entire stock of furniture, and had fared forth to the city to look for work and perchance, for the adventure that had passed her by.

Somehow the city, seen in anticipation, had seemed

flooded with chances for lovely adventure. She had read quantities of stories about country girls going to work in big offices and marrying the head of the firm and living happily ever afterward. She realized now that this was only fiction. She had found a job at once, even though it was a Depression year. The head of the firm had not shown any symptoms of falling in love with her. In fact, he was older than her father had been, and nearly as sweet and kind! Furthermore, the work that she did was routine, she was neither a trained secretary nor a book-keeper. It kept her so busy from morning until night that she had no time to think about, let alone find, romance!

For the first week or two in the city she had been so absorbed with the matter of self-adjustment, with learn-ing to work from nine to five, with making her few treasured belongings fit into a one-room apartment, that she had not found a moment in which to be lonely or bored. She had not found time to experience any grave lack, that is, not until the Christmas holidays had come round.

❄ ❄ ❄

The tree was nevertheless charming! Though the orna-ments on it had been purchased in a five-and-ten store, they were gay and bright and bursting with newness. Suddenly Clare, fastening them in place, wished that she had another pair of hands to help her. Of course, her father's hands were the ones she longed for at first. Swiftly she was remembering how large and muscular and helpful the hands of the unknown red-headed man had seemed. She had noticed them when he had given her his place in the car; he had raised his hat with one of them. Clare always noticed hands! They would be very nice hands to have around on Christmas, or on any other occasion!

I wonder if he'll pass by and see my tree from the street? Clare found herself thinking. *I wonder if it'll seem as adorable from the street as it does in here? Of course he won't know it's my tree, and yet I'd like to have him admire it. Perhaps I'd better skip downstairs and have a look at it from outside. Then I'll know exactly . . .*

Clare left the thought in midair, somehow it seemed so childish and silly; yet she found that, almost without her own volition she was struggling into her hat and jacket and starting down the two flights that led to the street.

She gained the street, a trifle breathless, and ran across the way to obtain a better view of her window. Looking up, eagerly, she found that her fears were groundless. For the little tree, standing in that window, was a sheer delight and a small glimpse of glory. As she stood on the sidewalk, head thrown back, staring at it, Clare was conscious of pride.

The pride must have shown from her face, for an old gentleman, passing by, paused beside her to look up. After a moment he spoke:

"I don't blame you for staring at that tree," he said. "Folks in cities don't have trees like they used to. That's the prettiest one I've seen in a week of Sundays. And, speaking of Sundays, it's a long time since we shared a pew—"

Clare turned to glance into a pleasant old face framed

with white hair. Yes, he was one of her few acquaintances, the old man whom she had met, so casually, in the church.

"I'm glad you like the tree," she told him, "because it's mine. You should see it from inside the room—it's even nicer than it is from down here. It was good of you," she added, "to remember that we'd met."

"I'd like to see it," said the old man, "and fancy forgetting you. You're far too modest."

"Why don't you come up to my room," she asked. "I know it's informal, but it isn't as if we were complete strangers. And, anyway, this is Christmas Eve and things should be informal on Christmas Eve."

"I'll say they should be. My name's Patterson," laughed the old man.

"I'm Clare Kimball. I'll make you tea and cinnamon toast, too," said Clare, growing excited, "that's what I'll do. We'll have a party, we two."

"It's a go," said the old man boyishly, and together they crossed the street and went up the two flights of stairs. Clare opened the door of her tiny home with an air of grandeur. The old man exclaimed, with a plentiful besprinkling of *oh*s and *ah*s, over her handiwork.

"This is the nicest thing that's happened to me for a long time," he said. "My little boy and I lead a kind of lonely life. We're from the country; we've been in town just a few months and things are still strange to us. Do you know, you're the first neighbor that I've called on since I've been here. My boy and I live down the line a way—"

Clare said, "If your boy is home, why don't you call him up—that is, if you have a phone—and tell him to drop in. I'll give him tea and toast, too—or milk, if he'd like that better. Little boys are usually bored with tea."

"He probably would enjoy a glass of milk," said the old man. Clare, looking at his elderly face, wondered about the boy of whom he spoke. *Maybe the child is his grandson,* she thought.

The old man went to the telephone and dialed a number. He moved quickly, eagerly. After a moment of waiting he spoke into the transmitter.

"Oh, Jim, I'm glad you're home," he said. "Say, if you'll drift down the street I'll introduce you to a lovely lady who has an elegant Christmas tree—to say nothing of," his smile was broad, "cinnamon toast."

A sputter of indistinguishable talk from the other end of the wire followed. The old man laughed and gave Clare's address. "It's on the second floor," he said, "come right up."

He replaced the receiver carefully and chuckled as he turned to Clare.

"You're a good Samaritan," he said, "taking in a couple of lonely souls on Christmas Eve."

"I was lonely myself," Clare told him. "You'd be surprised how lonely. You see, a few months ago my father died and I'm dreadfully alone in the world. A solitary feeling is awful at this season."

The old man reached out to touch her hand. "My wife died a few months ago, too," he told her. "Jim and I have been 'batching it' ever since. And, believe me, it's no fun. We don't like it!"

"Well," said Clare—she was busy laying out the teacups and setting a kettle on the gas plate that stood behind the screen—"Well, any time you two get lonesome, come in here and we'll cheer one another. I've had the identical experience you've had, and you're the first neighbor who has called on me. Cities aren't very friendly at first. At least, to country people."

The old man said: "It's fun to hear a kettle bubbling again. Jim and I eat in hotels or lunchrooms."

"It must be hard to get food for a small boy in restaurants," Clare said, "real nourishing food, I mean. Growing boys need all sorts of vitamins and calories and whatnot."

The old man laughed delightedly and slapped his knee. "Wait until you see my Jim," he said. "He's a growing boy, all right!"

Clare was slicing bread and mixing the cinnamon and sugar to be sprinkled over the bread when it had become toast. She plugged an electric toaster into the nearest socket. "Can I trust you," she said, "to see that the toast doesn't burn?"

"You certainly can," said the old man, "you can trust me implicitly!"

They worked together in a cheery silence for a space of minutes, the older man and Clare. A small dainty tea table was laid in front of the tiny gallant Christmas tree. Clare put out her best cups and saucers and the thin silver spoons that had been her grandmother's. She stood a rotund Santa Claus in the center of the table. "Your Jim will like that Santa," she said, thinking in terms of a little wide-eyed boy. The tea was quite ready when the buzzer sounded from downstairs. Clare ran to answer it.

"I wish I had some nice child to play with your son," she said, and again the old man laughed delightedly.

A clatter of feet came up the stairs and then a knock at the door. Clare, pink-cheeked and gay, flung the door wide and stood transfixed and puzzled. On the threshold stood the young man that she had seen so often, the red-headed young man of whom she'd been dreaming. In his large, capable hands, the hands that she had liked at first sight, he carried a cone of tissue paper that could only contain flowers.

"I stopped to get these for your lady friend, Dad," he began, and then his eyes rested on Clare's face. A slow flush started from his chin and mounted until it met his vivid hair. "Well," he said, "this beats the Dutch. Here I've been wanting to know you for a month, and wondering how I was going to put it over. And while I was wondering, my own dad up and beats me to it."

Clare replied, "From what your father said I thought you were a little boy, maybe eight or nine, or at best ten."

Mr. Patterson chuckled. "I know better," he said, "than to tell an attractive young woman that I've got an attractive young son. I wouldn't get any attention, myself, if I did. Girls always want to meet young men, nowadays. If I said, 'I've a son about your age,' you'd have said, 'Bring him up,' and I wouldn't have known whether you were a kind-hearted person, or just a somebody anxious to gather in a new beau. When I said, 'I have a little boy,' you wouldn't have invited him in unless you were the right sort. I guess I know my p's and q's. Oh, I'm an old deceiver, but I'll make it right with you one of these days!"

The red-headed young man was extending the flowers. Quite evidently he had not heard his father's speech.

"If I'd known," he said softly, "that it was you I'd have brought—"

The old man interrupted.

"Oh, say it, Jim," he laughed. "What you mean is you'd have brought mistletoe!"

Clare and the young man were speechless. Well, why should they not be? This is the beginning of their story, not the end.

Margaret E. Sangster, Jr.

Margaret E. Sangster, Jr. (1894–1981) was born in Brooklyn, New York. An editor, scriptwriter, journalist, short-story writer, and novelist, she was one of the best-known and most-beloved inspirational writers of the early part of the twentieth century.

Edith Ballinger Price

BOBO AND THE CHRISTMAS SPIRIT

In Red Rose Troop there were two forces always at work: Jane Burke's everlasting desire to do everything according to the book, and Bobo Witherspoon, as unpredictable and spontaneous as it's possible for any human to be.

And now Bobo was at it again.

❄ ❄ ❄

For ten long years this story has been clamoring to crawl inside Christmas in My Heart covers. I'm so sick and tired of its howling that I'm including it this year, just to shut it up.

*B*obo Witherspoon was forever upsetting the ordered life of Red Rose Troop—which, but for her, would have gone on almost entirely along the lines laid down for it by Jane Burke, who liked to do things according to a pattern. Bobo, being much the youngest member of the troop, was expected—quite naturally— to have no say-so in its doings. But whatever else she did, Bobo certainly did not live according to plan. Whatever pattern she followed was made as fresh as each day's dawn, and people with orderly minds like Jane Burke's simply cannot understand that sort of thing.

Therefore, when Bobo strolled in to the first autumn meeting of Red Rose Troop one particularly sultry September afternoon, singing *The First Noel*, it distinctly jarred on Jane's sensibilities.

"What on earth do you mean by that unseasonable yelping?" she demanded sharply.

Bobo looked pained. "It's just that I'm full of the Christmas spirit," she said.

Jane, Lillian, and Vera hooted at her in unison.

"Christmas spirit!" Jane cried. "I haven't recovered from Labor Day yet!"

Bobo looked distant and dreamy. "But it's there," she said. "I can get right into it any minute I want to. In fact, I have a hard time not being full of the Christmas spirit all year round."

"My dear child," Jane enunciated firmly, "we have hikes to consider just now. Hikes—and then the cookie sale, and our harvest party, and Thanksgiving, and—"

"And then Christmas," said Bobo softly.

"I think planning for the troop can safely be left to its

senior members," Jane remarked rather acidly. Time was fleeting.

But Bobo's singular obsession was persistent.

"Can't we do something about it?" Ruthie Kent complained to Jane a couple of weeks later. "She warbles *Deck the Halls with Boughs of Holly* while she pulls the cornstalks. She bawls *Jolly Old Saint Nicholas* while she cuts jack-o'-lanterns. It makes me feel as if I were going down too fast in an elevator."

Ruthie looked at her queerly.

"Good gracious!" cried Jane. "What was I singing?"

"*It Came Upon a Midnight Clear*," said Ruthie.

Jane clutched her brow in horror. "How can such things be?" she groaned. It was actually with some effort that she rallied herself and the troop to the work in hand. "Don't let your defenses down for a moment," she warned the others. "This thing is insidious."

So when Bobo arrived at the meeting a little before Thanksgiving, with a sprig of artificial holly in her buttonhole and a string of small bells jingling on her cap, Red Rose Troop bent determinedly over the cornshock they were arranging in a corner of the gym, and attempted to ignore her. But the bells pervaded the atmosphere with a frosty tinkle that was infectious.

"Jingle bells, jingle bells, jingle all the way!" hummed Red, tucking the pumpkin at the foot of the cornshock.

"Oh, what fun it is to ride in a one-horse open sleigh!" The troop took it up, and the room rocked.

"Stop it! Stop that immediately!" cried Jane. She cleared her throat and began to shout a counteractive strain.

The resultant discord was hideous. Jane stopped her ears and sang on with characteristic determination.

Bobo was not singing either ditty. She was sitting quietly in a corner, stitching away clumsily on a length of red muslin. It was not long before Jane spied her.

"And what is that, may I ask?" she demanded, taking her fingers out of her ears.

"Christmas stocking for an orphan," said Bobo promptly. "I have loads of the stuff. We can all make them."

"We are going to make scrapbooks," Jane announced, "for the children at the hospital."

"I thought it would be nice to make stockings," said Bobo, "and fill them with candies and jokes and things."

Several girls sat down near Bobo and inspected the pieces of red material that bulged from her workbag.

"What do you plan to put in these things?" Vera asked.

"Well," Bobo said, laying down her stocking for she could not possibly talk and sew at once, "I thought we could make some candy. And then, if we spent fifteen or twenty cents, we could get some little toys. And then we could make tiny little joke books with things cut out and pasted in, for each stocking—and put in some peanuts and popcorn, and things like a stringknitter or a puzzle."

"They'll have to be bushel baskets instead of stockings, won't they?" Lillian said.

Helen had picked up a length of red stuff and Bobo's scissors, and was chopping out a foot-shaped piece. She was absently humming *We Three Kings of Orient Are*. Red joined her, rummaging for thread, and soon half the troop was measuring and snipping and basting. Jane, her jaw set defiantly, advanced in solitary state upon the cornshock languishing in its corner, and put some ostentatious finishing touches to it.

But Bobo's great inspiration did not come to her until one day when she happened to be chatting with her friend, Mr. Horatio Bristle. No one else dared to chatter to Mr. Bristle; he had always cherished a reputation for being a rather formidable curmudgeon. Bobo's ability to wind him around her little finger never ceased to astonish her comrades. Always awed by him, they never got beyond, "Yes, Mr. Bristle," and "No, Mr. Bristle," if called upon to converse with him.

On this mild day of belated Indian summer the old gentleman was out in his garden, seeing if the half-hardy perennials were properly mulched, and admiring a few bronze chrysanthemums which had weathered the earlier frost.

"Ho, Bobo!" he called to his young friend over the fence. "D'ye like raw turnips? If you pull hard enough, I expect you can get one out of what's left of the vegetable patch."

Anything in the line of food appealed to Bobo. A raw turnip that has been touched by frost is a pungently appetizing affair. Bobo tugged one up, rubbed it off, and bit into it appreciatively.

Mr. Bristle eyed askance the one she pulled up and offered him.

"Hm, well," he mused, "I used to like 'em when I was a boy. After a day's gunning, I'd come across 'em in a field. Never will forget how good they tasted." He looked about him surreptitiously and took an experimental bite.

It was while they were thus engaged munching earthy turnips that Bobo's great thought came to her. "Mr. Bristle!" she cried. "I don't know why I've never noticed it before. Have you ever thought how much you look like Santa Claus?"

"Hey?" cried the astonished gentleman, choking over his turnip. "Santa Claus, did you say?"

"Yes!" exclaimed Bobo, her eyes growing rounder and rounder as she gazed. "Your face is so nice and red—and your mustache is so white. All you'd need would be a beard and the proper clothes. You're just the right shape—I mean, you wouldn't need any pillows or anything."

"Hrrumph!" snorted Mr. Bristle. "I wouldn't, hey?" He patted the front of his waistcoat rather ruefully. "Always meaning to do something about that."

"Oh, don't!" Bobo begged him. "You're just right. Oh, would you, dear Mr. Bristle—would you?"

"Would I what?" he asked suspiciously, backing away.

"Would you be Santa Claus when we go to the hospital to take the children their Christmas stockings?"

"*Me?* Santa Claus for a bunch of kids?" roared Mr. Bristle. "Jumping snakes, no! D'ye want Horatio Bristle to make an idiot of himself in public? If there's anything I can't abide—"

"It would just be poor little sick children who wouldn't have a proper Christmas," Bobo finished. "You'd only have to hand out the stockings. You wouldn't have to say anything."

"No!" said Mr. Bristle.

"Nobody'd even know who you were," Bobo assured him soothingly.

"No, no, NO!" shouted Mr. Bristle.

Bobo rummaged mournfully among the turnip tops. She began singing *God Rest You Merry, Gentlemen,* and then stopped.

"Go ahead, go ahead," said Mr. Bristle. "Sounds pretty. Takes me back."

"I can't go ahead," Bobo told him. "I was full of the Christmas spirit, but now that you won't be Santa Claus, I've sort of lost it all of a sudden."

"Christmas spirit—hmp!" snapped Mr. Bristle. "Feels more like Fourth o' July!" He picked a chrysanthemum and put it in his buttonhole.

"I can smell snow coming, though," sighed Bobo, "or I thought I could. And I could just see you in jolly red clothes, with a little bell on your cap. You do have such nice twinkly blue eyes."

"I suppose you'd like me to grow a beard by December twenty-fifth?" Mr. Bristle suggested, with what he intended for sarcasm.

"That would be wonderful!" cried Bobo. "Though I expect we could paste one on. Oh, then you will do it, Mr. Bristle? You *will!*"

"Never said any such thing!" stormed the outraged old gentleman.

"But you even said you'd grow a long white beard!" Bobo cried joyfully. "Oh, I do like you very much, Mr. Bristle, when you get co-operative!"

Mr. Bristle gnawed his mustache. "Well, Christmas is a long way off yet," he muttered evasively. "You never can tell."

"That's a real promise," Bobo interpreted, dancing gleefully in the turnip patch. "Well, good-by! I have to be very busy now, with lots of new plans. Don't really bother about the beard—we can make one."

She climbed over the fence and vanished.

Bobo won, though Jane Burke did her best to steady the situation and make everything conform to the original plan. But by the middle of December, Red Rose Troop was completely out of control. The first snowfall turned the trick. Bobo singing carols in September was sufficiently disturbing; Bobo frolicking in, her rosy cheeks flecked with snowflakes, was too much to withstand. The whole troop shouted *O Come All Ye Faithful* till the gym echoed. Jane sang along, too.

Bobo checked up on Mr. Bristle and found, to her delighted satisfaction, that he had obtained a handsome red suit and provided himself with a very becoming white beard which could be attached by means of hooks over his ears. He demonstrated it to her, and though the effect when seen with his gray business clothes and wing collar was quite surprising, Bobo approved wholeheartedly.

"Makes me look ten years older," sighed Mr. Bristle, detaching the whiskers and rubbing his pink chin.

"Oh, no!" Bobo assured him. "Younger, I think."

The troop was filled with mingled feelings of astonishment and gratification when Bobo made the spectacular announcement she had been saving up.

"Mr. Bristle is going to be Santa Claus, and hand out the stockings while we sing. Yes, truly—he's promised. And he has his red suit and a lovely woolly beard."

One helpful result of the announcement was that it

really finished Jane. She could not insist that the stockings be sent to the hospital, if the great Mr. Bristle, complete with red suit and whiskers, stood ready to distribute them.

On the morning before Christmas, Mr. Bristle called Bobo by telephone. "Lots o' nice snow piled up for you," he said. "I expect you're pleased. How're you planning to get over to the hospital?"

"Walk, I suppose," Bobo said. "Are your Santa Claus boots rubber ones, Mr. Bristle?"

"They are not!" he roared over the wire. "And Horatio Bristle isn't going to slip and slide through the streets of this town rigged up like that, anyway. How many of you are going?"

"About sixteen," Bobo figured.

"Well," said Mr. Bristle, "if you tell 'em all to meet at my house at five o'clock, I'll have something to convey us."

"Oh, ought you to?" said Bobo, who loved to walk in the snow. "Isn't it pretty skiddy?"

"Did you ever hear of Santa Claus using an automobile?" Mr. Bristle inquired.

"Oh, oh!" cried Bobo, breathless. "You—you don't mean reindeer, do you?"

There was a sort of choking sound from the other end.

At five o'clock, to Bobo's huge delight, snow was again falling softly through the blue winter darkness. No Christmas star—but then, you couldn't have stars and snowfall both at once, except on Christmas cards. Bobo sang as she ran to Mr. Bristle's house, and the bells on her cap jingled. She marveled that they should sound so loud, and so much as real sleighbells must sound. Some echo trick of the snow and the stillness, perhaps. Then, coming down the street, she saw dimly an enormous bobsled, drawn by two stout farm horses. The string of bells around the neck of each jangled rhythmically. She could see a group of Red Rose girls on Mr. Bristle's porch, peering out at the jolly sight, and she ran and joined them to watch the sleigh go by.

But it didn't go by. It pulled up with a hearty "Whoa!" at Mr. Bristle's gate, and the old gentleman himself, his white woolly beard bobbing above his ample crimson chest, came out of his house and looked about.

"Well, Bobo!" he cried, spying his young friend. "How d'ye like that? Hey? I knew just where I could get it, out in the country. Horatio Bristle didn't propose to wade around in the snowbanks—not to please anybody!"

Bobo was speechless. Miss Roberts said, "I think you must have caught the Christmas spirit, too, Mr. Bristle. We've all been exposed to it now for quite a long time."

"Christmas spirit, hmp!" said Mr. Bristle. But he beamed and chuckled every time he looked at the sleigh. It was a wonderful vehicle and it held all eighteen passengers, sitting on its floor in the sweet-smelling straw.

Mr. Bristle flourished his hand. "Hospital," he commanded.

The driver cracked his whip, and the wonderful, smooth motion began—the quiet gliding that is like no other motion in the world, broken only by the frosty jingle of the bells and the muted thud of the horses' hoofs on the snow. Quiet, that is, until Red Rose Troop began to sing. The Christmas spirit welled up within them till it hurt, and then they sang *Jingle Bells* as it should be sung. People, hurrying with wreaths and last-minute purchases, stopped to look and listen. What a sight it was—the big open sleigh, the two sturdy gray horses, the merry faces, and Santa Claus himself nodding and waving with abandon. Many of the passersby began to hum, themselves, as they hurried homeward.

"Funny," said Red. "You'd think we'd be there by now. Not that I ever want to stop sleigh riding."

"Horses are slower than automobiles," Jane reminded her instructively.

"Where are we, anyhow?" Vera wondered. It was difficult to see—darkness, and snow stinging the eyes that tried to penetrate it.

Just then there was a blur of light in the swirling flakes, and the sleigh pulled up before the dim bulk of a big hospital building. Everyone tumbled out and surged, stamping and blinking, into the entry.

"Let's park the stockings here," suggested Miss Roberts. "If the children see them first, we'll never be able to sing."

The red stockings were left beside the door, and then Red Rose Troop, still rubbing the snow and darkness from dazzled eyes, found itself suddenly in the bewildering brightness of a large rotunda. Miss Roberts opened her mouth to say they were expected in the children's ward—and it stayed open. The troop became dimly aware of boys in wheel chairs, boys on crutches, boys in maroon dressing gowns walking slowly about the rotunda. They were big boys, not children.

"Good gracious!" Miss Roberts gasped. "We're—we're at the Military Hospital! What shall we do?"

"Jumping snakes!" gulped Mr. Bristle. "I just said 'Hospital,' and this is what the driver thought I meant." He began to back towards the entrance door, grappling convulsively with his whiskers. Bobo caught him by his scarlet coat.

"What are you doing?" she whispered urgently. "Where are you going? We have to go on—oh, don't you see? They're all expecting us to!"

"But—" murmured Miss Roberts, looking apprehensively at all the eager grins, as more and more soldiers limped down corridors to the rotunda.

"Come on—come on!" begged Bobo desperately. "Oh, don't let them see we didn't mean it for them!" She began to sing *God Rest You Merry, Gentlemen,* and Red Rose Troop joined in, perforce.

Tenors and baritones came in, now—even Mr. Bristle's unexpected and apologetic bass.

There was clapping, and pleased laughter.

"Girl Scouts! Swell of them to come!"

"My kid sister's a Girl Scout. If I was home for Christmas . . ."

"And look at Santa! Gosh, no fake about him!"

There was an appreciative hum as the soldiers gathered around the carolers.

"Sing *The First Noel*—d'you know that one?"

"We'll come in on the chorus!"

"How about *O Little Town of Bethlehem?* We always sang that one Christmas Eve, at home."

So there was more singing—lots of it. Carols and marching tunes; and carols again. There was close harmony; there were barbershop chords; the deep voices joining with the troop's soprano melody gave the effect of a whole chorus. And Mr. Bristle found his tongue at last, and cracked jokes and told funny stories. And afterwards, every boy who could do so crowded near the door to see them off.

Outside, the snow had stopped and the stars shone like steel. One of the waiting horses tossed his head, and his string of bells clashed musically.

"I didn't dream it, then," said one boy softly. "Sleighbells! Like I was home in Minnesota."

"Gosh, we surely thank you for coming."

"It was kind of different from anything we've had—we sure appreciate it, ma'am."

"Do you guys remember where we were last Christmas?"

Someone said grimly, "Korea!" and there was a brief silence.

Mr. Bristle cleared his throat violently and cut a sort of caper on the steps. "Merry Christmas to all, and to all a good night!" he cried.

"Hi, Prancer! Hi, Dancer!" shouted one of the boys, as the sleigh pulled away. There was a cheer from the doorway.

Bobo, pulling the carriage robe to her chin, sighed blissfully. "Wasn't it simply wonderful?" she breathed.

"It turned out all right, I guess," Vera agreed. "There was a bad moment there at the beginning, though."

"It was perfectly simple," Bobo said earnestly, "as soon as everybody got the Christmas spirit."

Miss Roberts and Mr. Bristle exchanged looks.

"Seems to me it was you who made us go on with it, Bobo," Santa Claus remarked.

"No, I just started singing," Bobo said.

"It was certainly fortunate," said Jane, "that we left the stockings outside."

"I think it's too bad we did," Bobo said. "They prob'ly would have loved them."

"And then what would we have had for the children, pray tell?" Jane inquired. "For you may remember that we're still expected at the children's ward."

Bobo refrained from reminding Jane that her original plan had been merely to send scrapbooks. She was too busy thinking of the wonderful, unexpected adventure into which the Christmas Spirit had led them; of the pleased, touched faces they had just left behind, and of the small happy faces they would soon see.

"You are so nice, Mr. Bristle," she sighed, "when you get started. All those soldiers thought you really were Santa Claus. I know they did."

"Hm," said the old gentleman, smoothing his woolly whiskers, "by the time I've lived through this evening, I'll begin to believe I'm almost anybody except Horatio Bristle." But he chuckled.

The sleigh jingled on through the keen darkness of Christmas Eve. Everything was quiet, now, and the stars shone among the bare trees. Someone began to sing, very softly. "Silent night . . . Holy night . . ."

Bobo couldn't be sure, but it certainly sounded like Jane Burke.

Edith Ballinger Price

Edith Ballinger Price was born in New Brunswick, New Jersey in 1897. She was a poet, short-story writer, and novelist. Most of her writings were published during the first third of the twentieth century. *Blue Magic, Gervais of the Garden*, and *Ship of Dreams* are three of her more popular books.

Joseph Leininger Wheeler

WHITE WINGS

Far below the clouds she could see snowy mountains, glaciers, and serpentine rivers. Alaska!

Then the great silvery-white bird began its long descent into Fairbanks.

FAIRBANKS

Fairbanks was nothing she had imagined it to be, and everything she had not. She had imagined it to be frozen in ice and snow, complete with furred Eskimos, prospectors, and dogsleds. Instead, it was as if she'd been dropped into a medium-sized country town most anywhere in America. It was a warm summer day with no snow in sight. Flowers were in bloom everywhere—in pots, window boxes, and gardens. Fairbanks glowed with their vibrant colors. Just out of town, a paddlewheel steamboat plied the river. It was an unpretentious sort of town, its buildings and hotels plain and unassuming.

Night came, but someone forgot to tell the sun. It was late into the evening before a brief period of twilight gave lip service to night. It was the time of the midnight sun when darkness only visits for a few hours each night. The Arctic is an Alice-in-Wonderland world, with everything the reverse of what you expect. Only when she pulled closed the thick drapes in her hotel room and shut out the light could she finally drop into an exhausted sleep. Her dreams were troubled ones: the recurring theme had to do with a prisoner vainly trying to escape from a bleak maximum-security prison. The sound track consisted of mocking laughter echoing down endless halls of iron-barred cells. She woke, finding herself still exhausted.

ON THE RAILS

R-r-r-i-n-g! The sound of the alarm broke into Juliet's restless sleep. "Morning already!" she complained, but she knew she had to get out of bed or she'd miss the train.

Standing at the depot an hour later, she studied the

McKinley Express: long and glittering in blue and silver, with freshly washed Vista Dome glass—her home for the next two days. There was something about a train that had always called to her, wooed the long-caged restless spirit within her. Trains. Wings on rails to carry her far away from duties and responsibilities, from realities of a leaden hue.

Then the "All Aboard" sounded, and she climbed up the narrow stairway into the Vista Dome of her assigned car. Her suit of fine cashmere whispered wealth in spite of her modest demeanor. Finding a window seat about a quarter of the way down, she stowed her bag overhead and sat down. Watching the action outside and sizing up the passengers still boarding, she wondered how many others were in Alaska for the first time. Most passengers boarded in groups or in couples. Rare was the single, for most lone passengers had already clustered. She began to feel left out, a third thumb. Next-to-the-last to board was a man of average height, well-built, casually dressed, and topped off with a tan Tilley hat. As he approached the empty seat next to her, he paused indecisively, then moved on six rows to another empty seat. Surprisingly, she felt an unexplainable sense of loss.

There was a jolt, and the train was in motion. The crew was jolly, busy at their mission of transforming passengers into friends. First they took a roll call: Where was each passenger from? From everywhere, it seemed: a big batch from New York and New Jersey; another from various states in New England; and yet another from California; quite a few from Texas and Florida; four from Germany; three from Japan; two from South Africa; and one from France.

Breakfast was announced, and a porter came by to make up the tables. Three Jewish travel agents asked her if she'd like to be their fourth. It was a good beginning, for her companions were so friendly that she quickly shed her loneliness. The thawing process was evident at other tables as well. Breakfast tasted delicious, the upstairs crew doubling as their cooks and waiters.

Back under the Vista Dome, she found herself unable to read: the Alaskan wilderness was just too fascinating. The first moose (half-immersed in midriver) almost tilted the train off the rails as everyone rushed, cameras in hand, to that side of the tracks. But what impressed her most was the sheer immensity of the land contrasted by the scarcity of people. According to the crew, Alaska was both wonderful and lonely—especially lonely if you were one of those who lived in a house away from all roads, such as several homesteads they pointed out along the way. The crew seemed to know all the inhabitants by name, even where they had come from and how long they had lived there by the tracks, the railroad their only lifeline. In the seat just in front of her was a young couple and their two children, a son who was nine and a daughter, six. They hailed from Phoenix and planned to rough it for the summer in an isolated cabin. If they managed to stand it that long, they'd then decide whether or not to stay for the winter.

"Jack is tired of civilization," admitted Mary, his wife, "and he persuaded me to spend the summer up here— but I'm wondering if we haven't bitten off more than we can chew. There'll be no electricity, no indoor plumbing—it'll be life stripped of all but its bare essentials. Now the children," and here she looked at them fondly, "just consider it to be one big lark. . . . They don't realize that our diet'll be mostly fish." She sighed softly, but not loud enough for Jack to hear.

A little over three hours out of Fairbanks, the passengers were told to watch for their first sight of Mount McKinley—or *Denali*, "the Great One," as the Eskimos call it. Usually it was socked in by clouds, but who knew? They might get lucky this time.

But they didn't get lucky: Denali remained shrouded in her cloudy garments. So huge is America's highest mountain that it creates its own weather. Denali begins at only 1,000 feet in elevation then soars to 20,300 feet. The train stopped at Denali Station, where everyone boarded buses for the hotel complex.

At 3:30 that afternoon Juliet climbed into a light plane with three other passengers. Destination: Denali. The prospects of seeing the peak were slim, for the clouds were so high and dense. Yet at seventeen thousand feet the plane broke out of the mist—and there, directly in front of them, was the most awe-inspiring sight she had ever seen. It literally took her breath away. For perhaps fifteen to twenty seconds, the sun came out and transformed cold gray into blinding white crest, topped by the bluest of blue skies—then the vision disappeared, as the fog and rain closed in. But that ever-so-brief moment of beauty would be part of her always. Even the pilot, who'd been chattering virtually nonstop, became mute at the sudden apparition. They flew back to Denali Station in silence.

It rained all night.

It was still raining when they boarded the McKinley Express the next morning. This time, Tilley Hat (for so she had come to call him) stopped in the aisle next to her and politely asked if he could join her.

She smiled and nodded yes.

And so it began.

❄ ❄ ❄

After small talk came introductions. His name was Robert MacDonald, and he was a small-town newspaper editor from Granbury, Texas. Her name, he discovered, was Juliet Romano, and she owned and operated a shop in Aspen, Colorado. Christmas in the Rockies, it was called.

The ice broken, she laughed and said, "I've a confession to make."

"What's that?"

"I've been calling you 'Tilley Hat' in my mind."

"You *have?* . . . Most people don't even know this hat *has* a name."

"Well, I do, because my brother Richard has one. He maintains there's a kinship involved in its ownership— that no Tilley-hat wearers can be other than friends."

"True indeed. Just yesterday, in the Seattle airport, a fellow wearing a dark green one came up and introduced himself. Said he was visiting from South Africa, and had bought the hat at the factory in Canada. . . . And, I must confess, I had a name for you, too."

"Oh?"

"You'll probably think it strange, though."

"Why is that?"

"Well, I called you 'Madonna of Sorrows.' "

"Why?"

"Oh, I don't know. Perhaps because you have the soft, auburn-haired loveliness of a Raphael Madonna, and perhaps because you appeared to be so sad."

"Hmm—I didn't know it, uh, showed."

"Maybe it's because, being an editor, I'm used to studying people. . . . Their many moods, their personalities, what makes one different from another. Can tell what mood an employee is in before a word's been said."

Juliet didn't rise to the bait but merely admitted, "You may be right."

And he left it at that.

Right then the train began to slow, seemingly a hundred miles from nowhere. Questions were on everyone's faces. *Why here?* The family from Phoenix got up, Mary's face a blanched white: *This was it. Like it or not, she no longer had a choice.* The train stopped, then quickly started again . . . and there by the tracks, they stood waving. By their side were their belongings: their food, sleeping bags, tools, and other necessities—all they'd have to survive on for the next three months.

The day passed in a blur of mountains, trees, streams, birds, animals, isolated cabins, and hamlets. Juliet lost herself in the scenery, especially thrilled to spot a bald eagle, a fox, and two bears. Late in the afternoon, the train pulled into the depot of Anchorage, where nearly half the population of Alaska lived.

The next day, it seemed only natural that Juliet and Robert sit together on the bus to Seward, arriving at that seacoast village late in the afternoon. The town of Seward was named after William Henry Seward, who had served as secretary of state for both Abraham

Lincoln and Andrew Johnson. Seward had purchased Alaska from the Russians in 1867 for $7.2 million, making him the laughingstock of America. But with 20 percent as much land as the entire continental United States and stretching 2,600 miles, "Seward's Folly" was quite a bargain at only two cents per acre!

THE JUBILEE

In the harbor, looming out of the crystalline water like a great white swan, floated their ship, the *Jubilee*. This was to be their home for the next week. Fourteen years old, the cruise ship was 733 feet long, weighed 47,262 tons, carried almost 1,500 passengers, and was staffed by a crew of 670.

After checking in, and before going to their respective staterooms, Robert haltingly asked a question: "Juliet . . . , this ship is so large that we're not likely to see each other unless we plan now to do so. We're both traveling alone . . . and—uh . . . , speaking just for myself, the trip would be so much more enjoyable if I could share it with a friend. Do you think . . . uh—"

"Of course," she responded, "I'd like that too."

Thus they stood together on the top deck when the *Jubilee*, after several long blasts of its horn, majestically moved out of the harbor and into Blying Sound. They watched until the lights of Seward disappeared from sight.

Late that night, Juliet cuddled up in the well of her window, looking out at the moonlit water and listening to the waves slapping against the ship's hull. Too tired to think, she let her mind drift at will. About midnight, she dropped off into a dreamless sleep.

Very early the next morning she awoke to the same sounds: the low hum of the engine, the waves slapping the hull; and experienced the same slight roll of the ship. She smiled, sighed, and dropped back to sleep.

At 9 A.M., Juliet found her way down to the breakfast bar. Robert was already there at a table by the window, a large mug cupped in his hands. She couldn't remember the last time she'd faced a day with this much happiness.

Filled to capacity with breathtaking sights and scenery, the day passed quickly. They viewed the College Fjords as well as the fjords of Valdez, then took a small boat tour of the Valdez/Prince William Sound area, spotting wildlife everywhere—seals, otters, eagles, hawks, gulls. Juliet and Robert were both amateur photographers and naturalists, their friendship growing as the hours passed.

Inside the *Jubilee*, meals and snacks were available around the clock, and activities such as nature lectures, variety revues, quiz shows, musicals, films, games of chance, deckside sports, and shopping all added up to a ship that never slept.

That night a storm hit, and having left the sheltered bays for the open sea, the *Jubilee* was pounded by towering waves. But sitting by the rain- and wave-slashed window, Juliet reveled in the tempest. So long had she been assailed by inner storms that the external one she now experienced brought her nothing but a kind of primitive, savage joy.

In the morning, the sun out and storm gone, the ship moved through the vast snow-capped peaks of the

Wrangell-Saint Elias National Park (three times the size of Yellowstone).

As she and Robert scanned the magnificent mountain range with their binoculars, Juliet gasped as two sets of snow-white wings flashed into their line of vision—seagulls. For almost three hours the two gulls put on a performance neither Robert nor Juliet would ever forget: skimming the waves (only inches above the water), circling the ship, soaring so high above they were only blurs, yet always in sync, wings never touching, as choreographed as a ballet.

"Together, yet alone," mused Juliet. Then they were gone—never to be seen again.

Then came quieter waters, and the famous Hubbard Glacier. The great ship drew as near as the captain dared, then stopped in the midst of a field of small icebergs. Mesmerized, the passengers watched the *calving*: office-building-size sections of ice breaking off and crashing into the sound. Both Robert and Juliet had seen this phenomenon in film a number of times, but to actually experience it firsthand was something else entirely! Each time, there was a crack of thunder followed by the slow-motion fall of a new iceberg and a great splash of milky water. Juliet pulled her scarf tightly around her neck, for the wind coming off the glacier chilled her to the bone.

Historic Skagway was next, the jumping-off point for the Klondike Gold Rush of 1898. Juliet and Robert took the train to the top of Chilkoot Pass. It was here that almost thirty thousand prospectors were forced by the Canadian government to haul up two thousand pounds of provisions each before they were permitted to go on to the Yukon. That meant that each prospector had to find a horse with stamina enough to make it to the top with a hundred pounds of supplies a minimum of twenty times! Not surprisingly, over three thousand horses died here. And those unfortunate prospectors who couldn't afford to acquire horses were forced to carry two thousand pounds of provisions to the top on *their own shoulders!*

TWO STORIES

Lovely Juneau, accessible only by sea, was next. Of all the towns and cities they saw, they loved Juneau most. As they had up and down the Alaskan coast, Robert and Juliet marveled at the pristine water, the almost complete absence of pollution and urban sprawl—America as it once was.

They'd seen so many floatplanes taking off from the waterways that they finally chartered one. What an experience! The view of mountains, lakes, glaciers, rivers, and fjords was breathtaking. During the afternoon, they landed on several glaciers and one remote lake. On the shores of this crystalline lake they saw two grizzly cubs, a wolf pack, and half a dozen bald eagles. It was a Shangri-la most difficult to leave. They made it back to the *Jubilee* with only twenty minutes to spare. As the white floatplane took off again in the late afternoon sun, Juliet thought, *White wings. If only I had white wings to take me away from everything!*

That evening, after dinner, both Robert and Juliet were quiet and contemplative, each lost in their own thoughts. Finally, Juliet broke the ice: "I see that you're wearing a wedding band, and can't help but wonder

why you're here on this beautiful ship all alone."
Robert hesitated before answering.

"I'm afraid you won't find my story to be a happy
one, Juliet. I'm Texas-born and grew up in south Fort
Worth. My father was a minister and my mother a stay-
at-home mom. My childhood was, by and large, happy,
and my parents' marriage a solid one. I've always loved
books and writing, thus I majored in journalism and
history at Texas Christian University. Along the way I
fell in love with a lovely blonde from Dad's church. A
prom queen, she was the campus dream girl. Somehow,
I don't know how or why, she chose me over the
others.

"Seven years went by. Gloria was happy in her nurs-
ing job but yearned to have a child . . . , but no child
ever came to us. It about broke my heart too, for I also
felt incomplete without children in the house.

"We both attempted to compensate for the child void
by becoming workaholics. Gloria took extra shifts at the
hospital and I stayed late at the newspaper. A friend of
Dad's had owned the *Granbury Tribune* and he brought
me aboard as assistant editor after I graduated from
Texas Christian. Eventually Gloria and I saved enough
money for a down payment on the paper, paying the
rest on time. The *Tribune* became the child we couldn't
have. Immersing myself in the community, I joined
Rotary and Kiwanis, as well as being a director of the
Chamber of Commerce. The paper grew, as most
anything does if you give it your all.

"But, needless to say, none of this strengthened our
marriage. We began to drift apart. We had a long talk
and decided to attend a marriage encounter weekend

sponsored by our church. There—that weekend—we realized how close to divorce we had drifted. We renewed our vows. Then we packed our things and headed home."

There was a long pause while he struggled for control. . . . Finally, he picked up the thread of the story again:

"It was night, on the road south of Fort Worth—we'd just passed Cresson, when around the corner came a pickup truck out of control, going way too fast to hold his curve trajectory. I hope you never experience that utterly helpless feeling of seeing two headlights in the opposing lane cross the yellow line heading dead center for you. Because of the speed, there was no chance in the world of getting out of the way, and to jerk the wheel would be to flip our SUV. Nor was there time for the proverbial replay of one's life you hear about in such situations, only for Gloria's 'Bob, Bob! He's going to—' and then the deafening crash. The pickup's horn was stuck on. With that terrific impact I felt certain the next face I saw would be the good Lord's. But no, I was still alive and aware. Checked my left foot—it moved. Same for the right. Same for each hand. I was in tremendous pain, gasping for breath and crying. But hearing nothing from Gloria, I turned—and wished I hadn't."

"Oh!"

"Yes, she'd taken more of the hit than I. True, her airbag deployed, but the impact was so great that she was pushed halfway into the back seat. I could hear her whimpering, making gasping noises."

Again he paused for control then continued.

"A doctor just behind us saved her life. Called an

ambulance on his cell phone, and we were rushed to a Fort Worth trauma center. Gloria was wheeled into the operating room. Had the best surgeon in the city. But nothing he could do was enough."

"She *died*?"

"No, but what happened to her was worse than death. So many vertebrae were crushed that she was paralyzed from the neck down. And since her trachea received such a direct hit, she lost the use of her voice as well."

"Oh no!"

"Yes, she, my once-lovely Gloria, only twenty-nine years of age, is now completely helpless. Brain still functions—and eyes. But nothing else does—or ever can."

"Oh! Oh!" was all that Juliet could say.

"So there she lies in her hospital bed, in what used to be our bedroom, or in the front room by the window that overlooks Lake Granbury—that's where I wheel her when I go to work. A nurse watches over her while I'm at the *Tribune*. I come home twice a day to check up on her. She gets her food through tubes."

"And absolutely no hope?"

"None whatsoever."

"And you've had no communication whatsoever with her for—for . . . how long?"

"Six and a half years. The *only* communication is through her pain-wracked eyes and occasional answering pressure in one hand. Just imagine what it would be like to be locked in a body that refuses to obey the brain! That's the worst of it: she *knows* what has happened to her, and she *knows* what has happened to

216

me. I'm certain she wishes herself dead . . . , but she's strong—strong in spite of her broken body."

"And the driver of the pickup?"

"That's the part of the story I've had the hardest time with—he got out of it with hardly a scratch. And he'd been going close to a hundred miles an hour, according to the police report."

"And her expenses?"

"Had to take the driver and his insurance company to court. A settlement finally, just last year, paid her medical bills—$850,000 at last count, paid her lawyer, and left me enough to get by, but only if I keep her there at home."

"I admire you. Not many men would have stayed by her."

"Well, I made vows to stay by her *in sickness and in health, in good times and in bad, till death do us part*— repeated those vows to both God and man—*twice*. . . . And death has not parted us."

"But *how* have you coped with it? Haven't you become angry and embittered or lost faith in God?"

"Oh I'll admit to some dark days, and even darker nights, there in that house, as silent as a tomb. And I've cried till I have no more tears to weep. Begged God to call her home to Him. I know she's ready to go. Asked God about me too: would I ever again have a companion, a wife? Was I doomed to celibacy for life, in my mid-thirties? It's been hard, Juliet, awfully hard."

"So how did you get *here*?"

He smiled for the first time. "Well, I still felt bound to the Gloria that once was and have had a very difficult time accepting the fact that I'll never have that Gloria back again. Gradually it began to get to me, and my health began to suffer. I became more irritable at the office. After having been generally cheerful all my life, I sank deeper and deeper into despondency. In fact, it got to the point where Mom and Dad began to fear for my life. They came over to the office one afternoon and handed me a long envelope. When I opened it, there was a ticket for this Alaskan cruise."

"What wonderful parents you must have!"

"Yes, I'm blessed. . . . They furthermore said not to worry: they'd watch over Gloria while I was gone."

"Oh my!"

"And what does 'Oh my!' mean?"

"Oh, I wish I'd known all this earlier."

"What good would *that* have done?"

"Guess it wouldn't have."

"And if you had, you might have been nice to me just because you felt sorry for me. I wanted you to like me for myself alone."

"I *do* like you for yourself alone. . . . I just wish there was more I could do to assuage your pain."

"I can tell that you truly understand," said Robert. "And that means a lot to me. I strongly suspect you've experienced more than your fair share of pain as well. How did you end up on this cruise all alone?"

"Well, I was born in Monterey, California. My father owned a beachfront hotel there, and my mother helped him run it. I'm one of three children. I grew up happy. Well, I *was* happy until the day Dad told Mom he'd met someone he loved more than her. It happened the day after I graduated from high school. It shattered Mom. She was never the same happy mother after that. She took Dad to court; it was a long and angry trial, and she saw to it that all Dad's dirty laundry was hung out to dry on the Monterey clothesline. In the end, she got half—Dad had to sell the hotel. Mom bought a mansion on Carmel's Seventeen Mile Drive, and there she exists today. I can't really call it living—still angry and bitter after all these years. I can't be in her house for more than twenty-four hours without going bonkers. I've never had a home to go back to since, for Dad dropped out of my life completely."

"How sad!"

"I packed my things two days after graduation, cleaned out my savings account, and moved north to Santa Cruz, where I got a job waiting tables at a restaurant; later on, I enrolled at the University. Majored in Psychology. Perhaps because I was so mixed up myself. Got my bachelor's degree, and halfway toward my master's I met Max. He was drop-dead handsome, smooth, worldly, well-to-do, and considered to be the catch of the campus."

"And you decided to remove him from circulation?"

"Oh, I wasn't quite *that* calculating." She laughed. "The truth of the matter is that I was terribly lonely and tired of being poor and waiting tables. So when he told me how beautiful he thought I was and offered to take me 'away from all this,' I accepted, with stars in my eyes and hope in my heart. We married that very night. Justice of the peace. And honeymooned in Spain."

"Didn't want a church wedding?"

A shadow passed over her face. After a pause, she continued, in a very low voice: "*I* did, but he didn't. I had attended church up until my parents' divorce, but I was so angry at God for letting Dad walk out on us that I'm afraid I gave God up at the same time. But I missed that dimension in my life and hoped I'd marry a Christian, and thus have an excuse to attend church again.

"But, as you see, I married Max instead. And he's never felt any need for God. Only money. And he's made lots of it: bought and sold hotel after hotel, making money each time, until he finally bought the five-star hotel he owns in Aspen now."

"*He* owns?"

"Yes, *he.* . . . Had me sign a prenuptial agreement to that effect. I was too naïve then to fully realize what I was signing. It was years before I finally woke up to the realization that everything but the house was all his."

"Did . . . you have children?"

"Yes, thank the good Lord. Three: a boy and two girls—nine, six, and four, respectively. They are my comfort."

"Oh?"

"Yes, I'm sure you're aware by now that I'm *still* a lonely woman. Max gives me plenty of money; bought the Christmas store for me. Laughingly said, 'Go and play with your toy—it'll get you out of the house.' But he doesn't give me much else. I try to be a good wife to him, entertain his clients, never reject his conjugal demands if I can possibly avoid it. If I do, he gets angry and gives me the silent treatment for weeks at a time. But in spite of all this, he—he—has not been faithful to me."

"And yet you stay?"

"Of course! True, I didn't make my vows in front of God in a church. But in my heart, I promised God I

would. Since our marriage, I've attended church whenever I possibly could, for I've needed God so. I take the
children with me. Max deeply resents our going, and
usually has something cold and biting to say about it,
but we go anyway. But it's hard, because there are so
few churches in Aspen. Grocery stores either. The reality is that Aspen is nothing more than palatial homes
empty for all but a few weeks of the year, with the average home cost now approaching $3½ million. It's *not* a
family town, and few marriages last long there. So I
have to go clear to Glenwood Springs to find a church.
And I have almost no real friends in Aspen—other than
my employees at the Christmas shop."

"I had no idea Aspen was like that."

"Oh, I haven't told you the half of it! It's not just the
transient super-rich who float in and out with their
chauffeurs, butlers, maids, nannies, and servants. It's also
the people who stay in hotels like Max owns—where
the nightly rates are stratospheric. Even at that, many
stay weeks at a time, in suites. From what I've seen,
however, a good share of them are miserable in spite
of all their wealth. Why, just two weeks ago, a woman
screamed out to the front-desk manager—could be
heard throughout the entire floor, 'Just because I'm the
second richest woman in America, you've no business
overcharging me!' Yes, she made *quite* a scene."

"They're not *all* like that, are they?"

"No, of course not, but if one may judge by Aspen,
it's clear that money certainly doesn't bring much
happiness. Without work, life has no purpose."

"So how do *you* find happiness?"

"Through my children, through work at the store, and through God."

"Not through Max?"

"No. Oh let me qualify that. I think he loves me in his own way. He's a child of divorce too. His parents gave him all the money he wanted and none of the love; that's why I don't know if he's even capable of true love. Since he wasn't given it at home, apparently he's incapable of passing it on."

"And the children?"

"Oh, he's proud of them and pets them if they're well behaved and don't get on his nerves. Heaven help the one who does!

"As for me, I don't think he's likely to divorce me—not as long as I keep my looks, that is. He considers divorce to be . . . uh . . . *messy* is his word for it. As it is, he has the best of all possible worlds: a wife who loves him far more than he deserves, children who both admire and fear him, employees who tremble at his every word, and women who fawn over him. He travels all over the world. . . ."

"But doesn't take you?"

"But *never* takes me—says my place is with the kids."

"So, how did *you* get here?" he grinned.

"Funny you'd ask. It's this way. Guess I was looking kind of down. One night, when he'd been in Tahiti for most of a month—at least I *assumed* he was in Tahiti, as he rarely calls me, everything sort of caved in on me at once: the realization that our marital love was so one-sided, that I was 'safe' only as long as I accepted his infidelities and coldness, and as long as I kept my youth and looks. So there in our 15-million-dollar mansion,

envied by most everyone who doesn't know me well,
coveting the love some of my poorer married friends
take for granted, I cried out to God: 'Oh Lord, it's all so
hopeless! There's no light at the end of my tunnel, only
dark and more dark. I don't know how I can take it any
longer. I'm not asking out of my marriage—I walked
into it with my eyes wide open. And I don't want my
children to experience the desolation and rejection I did
when Dad walked out of our home. No, all I ask, Lord,
is for *hope*—hope that my life will not always be dark.
And a friend, a true friend who'll accept me just the way
I am. Unconditionally. A friend who'll cherish me and
tell me I'm worthy of friendship. A friend who'll walk
into my life—and stay. Give me a sign, Lord, that you
haven't forsaken me!' I cried myself to sleep that night."

"You poor soul!"

"Two days after that prayer, I received a cablegram
from Max. And here it is." She reached into her purse
and unfolded a yellow piece of paper that had obviously
been read and reread a number of times. This is what it
said:

> *Dear Juliet,*
>
> *Still in Tahiti. Bored stiff. Home Tuesday. Today's
> your birthday, and I forgot to give you anything. You're
> such a good wife, better perhaps than I deserve. Take ten
> thousand or so and go on a cruise to somewhere. You've
> never gone anywhere. I'll take care of the children this
> time. Go!*
>
> *Love, Max*

"Unbelievable!" muttered Robert.

"Isn't it? So, as I always wanted to go to Alaska, I was able to get the ticket for this cruise."

"And Max, do you think he's changed?"

"Well, I thought perhaps he had, but on his return, he was the same old Max, a bit disgruntled, in fact, at what he'd let himself in for. If you want the real truth, I think he'd been afraid my unhappiness would end up aging me." She laughed. "It most likely *was,* so it'll probably turn out to be an astute business investment for him after all."

"So God answered your prayer?"

"Yes, bless Him! . . . And He even brought me that friend: you! You fully understand that friendship is all I can offer, for both of us have made vows before God. But you and I both know that friendship is one of the greatest gifts God can bestow, for without true friends, how could any of us make it through this thing called life?"

"Isn't that the truth?" replied Robert.

WHITE WINGS

The next day it was on to Ketchikan, aglow in the ultramarine. They shopped and went out on a small boat looking for birds—and found them. Saw the salmon flailing their way up the river in which they were hatched, their God-given instinct driving them up the river to spawn and die.

"How do they *know?*" Juliet wonderingly asked him.

"According to a fisheries executive I spoke with in Juneau," Robert answered, "it's some quality, some unique chemical element in the river itself that calls to them thousands of miles out in the Pacific—calls and summons them home to the mouth of the river, up the river, no matter what obstacles stand in the way, to the very spot in which they hatched. Only then do they spawn. Only then can they relax, give up the long fight, and die."

"What a God we have!"

❊ ❊ ❊

Then the great white swan spread her wings and they were off to the Inside Passage. Every hour now, every minute, every second, tasted bittersweet, for up ahead in the clouds they could sense the southern terminus of their island in time.

The next day—their last day together—as they stood watching whales cavort and blow on both sides of the ship, Robert pensively asked her if he might leave a very special gift with her.

"Of course!"

"Well, Juliet, it's really a gift from God—and it alone has given me the courage to face each day."

"Whatever it is, I need it too. . . . Go ahead."

"Are you familiar with David's Psalm 139?"

"I don't think so. Please share it."

"Very well. I've memorized the parts that mean the most to me:

> *O Lord, you have examined my heart*
> *and know everything about me.*
> *You know when I sit down or stand up.*
> *You know my every thought when*
> *far away.*

You chart the path ahead of me
and tell me where to stop and rest.
Every moment you know where I
am.
You know what I am going to say
even before I say it, Lord.
You both precede and follow me.
You place your hand of blessing on
my head. . . .

You watched me as I was being
formed in utter seclusion,
as I was woven together in the dark
of the womb.
You saw me before I was born.
Every day of my life was recorded in
your book.
Every moment was laid out
before a single day had passed.

Psalm 139:1-5, 15-16 NLT

"I'd never heard that before. Would you mind repeating it once more for me?"

He did. Then there was a long silence, broken finally by Juliet:

"Reminds me of a passage in C. S. Lewis's *Mere Christianity*. In it, he maintains that since God is not in time as we are, He sees us as a vast tree, with the past connecting the present to the future—each of us interacting with each other according to His divine master plan."

"In other words, God is a sort of Grand Chess Master or Master Choreographer?"

"Precisely."

"Nothing takes place, even casual conversations, by mere chance?"

"True."

There was a long pause, then Robert thoughtfully observed, "If all this is true, then God put me on that train and on this ship—and put you on board as well, just because He loves us both and wants to comfort us, give us the courage to carry on back home."

"True on all counts."

❄ ❄ ❄

It was the last night of their island of time, and the full moon silvered the waters of the Inside Passage. Here and there, off to either side, twinkled lights from homes, graphic evidence that the Last Frontier lay behind them and civilization ahead of them. Mesmerized, they watched silently as the great shadowy prow of the *Jubilee* sliced through the dark waters below, phosphorescent billows sweeping away on either side, and only the sounds of night birds breaking the serenity of the night.

Others, too, realizing how soon civilization would displace this quiet beauty, stood by the railing, drinking in the night. Eventually, close to sixty, including wide-eyed children, made up the company.

Just before they returned to their rooms, Juliet spoke these words: "Robert, I'm so grateful God brought you into my life. Brought someone who didn't pressure me to give what I'm not free to give. Someone to reassure me that I, too, am a child of God and that God knows the dark road I must tread. Knows, empathizes, and understands. And that God loves me.

"Because of this, Robert, I now have the courage to return to a house that is cold, to a man who loves me little, and to children who love me much. You've helped me believe in myself again, Robert. Believe that God has a plan for the rest of my life. Psalm 139 gives me special comfort. Never will I feel truly alone again."

There was a long silence before Robert responded, "I don't want you to feel the benefits of this trip have been one-sided, Juliet. You'll never know how much you have comforted, encouraged, and strengthened me. I feel I can now return to a house where the shadows never seem to lift—and try harder to lift them." His voice broke on that last phrase.

Then he prayed the Lord's blessings on them as they went their separate ways only hours from then.

Next morning, after promising to stay in touch, they bade good-bye to each other, not at all sure they'd ever see each other again.

❄ ❄ ❄

That December, Robert received a long letter, on seagull stationery. It began with these words:

> *Christmas in the Rockies*
>   *Dear Robert,*
>
> *It's almost Christmas, and the children and I have deco-rated our house, emphasizing Christ rather than Santa. I read Christmas stories to them every night—how they*

look forward to it! Max neither understands nor approves,
but we make our own happiness.

How often I have relived my trip to Alaska. How
often I have seen again the white-winged plane from
which I caught that one glorious glimpse of Denali; that
white-winged seaplane that carried us to that remote lake,
where I wanted to stay; that white-winged swan named
the Jubilee, and the two white-winged gulls off the
Wrangell-Saint Elias coast. How I envied them their
freedom, and how I yearned to follow them. But you
helped to teach me a great lesson: life is not that simple.
We are never free to live a life dedicated to self. Like it or
not, each of us is connected—connected to parents, brothers, sisters, aunts, uncles, grandparents; connected to
husband, wife, children, friends, and community. Like
that phosphorescent wake we watched that last night on
the Jubilee, each word we say, each act, each decision of
our lives, leaves its wake—and that wake rolls on and on
into eternity itself. So, though we may fly like the gulls,
we're never free. No freer than God Himself, who created
us and then is stuck with us for all time.

So, should we disregard all this and turn our backs on
the impact of our actions and words on those who love,
depend on, respect, and admire us, then the consequences
would likely be far greater than any brief high we might
have felt during the breakaway. The cost would be far too
high.

A few days from now, you'll receive a package. I first
saw it in a shop in Juneau. For this limited edition, a
master carver created two soaring, snow white gulls, wings
spread in flight. Their wings do not touch, can never
touch, as they are frozen this way for all time. One

sculptured piece stays with me always; the twin goes to you. May God grant you and yours a Christ-filled Christmas.

❊ ❊ ❊

It was two days before Christmas when his package reached her. In it was a two-page letter:

Granbury, Texas
  Dear Juliet,

Received your wonderful present. Nothing could possibly have brought me more joy! Have placed it on our fireplace mantel where we can both see it every day. While noth-ing has changed in this house, I've taken it upon myself to change the atmosphere. I too have decorated the house for Christmas in a lavish way, even with the crèche I used to put up at Christmas. When I positioned it on a small table where Gloria could see it, the closest thing to a smile I've seen on her face in seven years appeared, and the dull stare temporarily left her eyes. I even play Christmas CDs for her. And—you'll laugh. . . . No, on second thought, you won't—I even read Christmas stories to her. Nothing is wrong with her hearing. In the Kingdom, I'll ask her what she thought of them. Our conversations on the ship gave me the courage and joy to change the atmosphere in the house: to show Gloria that I love and respect her still, even if she can no longer artic-ulate that she yet loves me too.

  And I have a present I hope you'll like. I'm no poet, but I wrote this poem for you, then copied it onto parch-

ment paper. My copy will remain on my office wall. Just as is true with your copy, two snow white seagulls have been painted against the Alaskan sky and the Jubilee.

White Wings

Far far north in the land of the midnight sun,
We saw two seagulls with snow white wings.
Together, yet alone; never saw them touch
As they serenely floated down the air rivers of the sky.
How my heart yearned to be a gull like they:
Free to soar into Alaska's azure sky,
Free to roam far out to sea,
Free to stand on Mount Elias's crest.
Could I but be freed from the trials of my life,
The coldness, the never-ceasing anguish;
Freed from the squirrel cage of spiraling darkness,
Spinning, ever spinning, but never a ray of light.
The Lord answered my heartfelt plea
By sending me a white-winged gull
Who floated with me down the air rivers of the sky,
Who sang with me the joy of life.
Now that I have returned to my squirrel cage,
Now that I have shouldered once again my cross,
All is changed, for there on my mantel
Are two snow white gulls:
Together—yet alone.

❄ ❄ ❄

HOW THIS STORY CAME TO BE

I've always been fascinated by the story behind a story: the gestation of it, how much of it actually happened.

I've discovered that many, if not most, of our readers share that fascination. I've also discovered that God has a way of putting to use every last thing that has ever happened to us—including rabbit trails and dead-end roads.

Like everyone else, a writer goes through periods. My most recent one resulted from the mix of stories I've been putting together for WaterBrook/Random House; subject: Tough Times. Stir into the mix one of the most powerful sermon stories I ever heard, by Louis Venden. In it, he points out that eleven of the twelve Apostles died violent deaths, and that God does not normally reward our "good works" with happily-ever-afters—that joy and pain go hand in hand in life, with pain predominating. Also, in recent weeks and months, more and more true stories (some involving people I know personally) have surfaced: men, women, and children who bravely make the best of it out of pain and heartbreak. Thus the conviction came upon me that perhaps at least some of my stories ought to reflect this ever-present reality. "White Wings" is the first such story I've written since the co-authored "Luther" story in *Christmas in My Heart 4.*

So it was that seventy-two hours ago, on the upper deck of our Colorado home, high in the Rockies, and with squirrels and chipmunks scampering, and birds flying all around me, I sat down with a blank piece of paper in front of me. Then, as I always do before I write, I prayed to my Lord (who never spoke without stories when He walked this earth): "Lord, on this so beautiful day that You've granted to us, I ask You for a gift: Get rid of Joe Wheeler and fill me with You. Let what I write not be my story but Yours. Give me a story that You feel needs to be told and that will be both a blessing and a source of courage to those who read it. Happy, sad, or both, I'll accept whatever plot You give me."

Then I leaned back and waited. Within ten minutes the Lord had given me this story; let me qualify that: had given me the beginning and the protagonists. I wouldn't know until the seventy-two hours had passed what would happen to them or how the story would end.

The catalyst was our first-ever (but, hopefully, not last) cruise—to Alaska last fall, for our wedding anniversary. This story would not have happened without that cruise. The wreck scene was taken from our February 25 head-on collision, when a speeding driver smashed into us. But we were luckier than were Robert and Gloria in this story because we have healed almost completely. Granbury I knew well for fourteen years. As for Aspen, two autumns ago Connie and I stayed one night, at off-season rates, in one of that resort town's grandest hotels. I overheard the tirade of the "second richest woman in America" myself. Had a long discussion with the maître d' about it and about what it was like to serve America's super-rich. And the prototype for Robert is my father-in-law, Derwood Palmer, who, when his wife of over half a century, Vera, experienced a massive stroke and was no longer able to communicate except by a squeeze of the hand, to move any part of her body, or to control her bodily functions, tenderly and lovingly took care of her in their home for almost five years. When we asked him how he stood it, he said, "It's not hard—when it's your girl."

When Mom died, Dad didn't have any tears left: he'd cried all he had already. As for the role of friends and soulmates in our lives, I've been mulling that over ever since I put together *Heart to Heart Stories of Friendship* (Focus on the Family/Tyndale House, 1999). I could not even imagine a life devoid of the cherished friendships that so enrich, encourage, and bless my life! We live in such a dissolute society that deep friendships between men and women, men and men, and women and women are all twisted into evil by those who have ceased searching for innocence and goodness in others (though it is also true that married people must take care, lest emotional intimacy with a nonspouse damage their marriage or lead to other, forbidden intimacies). And that's one of the tragedies of our time, for one of God's greatest gifts to us is friendship. He is indeed the Author of all true and abiding friendships.

As for the poem, "White Wings," God withheld that from me until the morning after the story came to its close.